PZ 7 P54 Th

Phillips, Louis
Theodore Jonathan Wainwright is going to bomb the Pentagon

THEODORE JONATHAN WAINWRIGHT IS GOING TO BOMB THE PENTAGON

a comic novella
by Louis Phillips

Prentice-Hall, Inc.,
Englewood Cliffs, N.J.

Theodore Jonathan Wainwright Is Going To Bomb The Pentagon
by Louis Phillips

Printed in the United States of America • 2

Prentice-Hall International, Inc., London
Prentice-Hall of Australia, Pty. Ltd., North Sydney
Prentice-Hall of Canada, Ltd., Toronto
Prentice-Hall of India Private Ltd., New Delhi
Prentice-Hall of Japan, Inc., Tokyo

Library of Congress Cataloging in Publication Data

Phillips, Louis.
Theodore Jonathan Wainwright is going to bomb the Pentagon.

SUMMARY: An eighteen-year-old college freshman is preoccupied with his plans for entering the first National Collegiate Elephant Race and bombing the Pentagon.

[1. Humorous stories] I. Title.
PZ7.P54Th [Fic] 72–10212
ISBN 0–13–913004–7

For Pat

1

Monday, October 2

Monday, two days after we decide to bomb the Pentagon from the air, it is raining. I should have counted on it, for it's all part of the conspiracy.

Take Peace Marches, for example. There hasn't been one where it hasn't rained. There may have been a couple where it only drizzled, and there may have been one somewhere where it didn't rain. But for the most part you have to admit that rain and Peace Demonstrations go together. Last week, for example, Lew Kemp and I organized a march against War—Capital *W*, yes sir. We organized a march against killing and atrocities, and against napalming women and children, and some local aviator took it upon himself to seed the clouds. By the time those clouds let go, Noah himself wouldn't have turned out. I know I'll never live to see such a downpour again. But then I don't know how long I'm going to live anyway. Maybe it's better to die young and be spared all this misery. I was in the fifth grade when my teacher first used the word "pessimistic" on me, and I didn't even know what it meant. I do now though. That's what learning's all about.

Naturally, on the day of the Peace March, with seven or eight inches of rain falling, nobody, but nobody, showed up. I've seen more participants at a volleyball festival. I showed up, of course, and Lew Kemp came with some girl he'd met. Her name is Mary Poppins. At least that's what Lew called her. But aside from them no one else came. We walked a couple of blocks in the downpour, chanting "HELL NO, WE WON'T GO" and "BRING THEM HOME NOW." All the while the sheriff sat in his patrol car and laughed his head off. He had a right too, I guess, because the three of us looked pretty ridiculous. Actually there were more than three of us, but not too many more, so it doesn't make any difference. Dr. Jelleff, my Medieval History professor, stood on the sidelines and offered me his umbrella but I turned it down. I didn't want to get him in trouble with the school. Finally we had to choose between drowning and going home. So I went back to my dormitory. Lew and Mary went off by themselves. The rain stayed right where it was for a long long time.

October 2—later

I suppose I should be angry. I should make a fist and shake it at the sky, cursing Dow Chemical and swearing at all those guys who seed the clouds. An entire Peace Parade washed down the drain. And yet, the more I think about it, the more I understand the nature of The Conspiracy against dissent. Nobody wants to hear anyone say no. It's yes, yes, yes, yes. It's been happening that way all over the place—England, Ireland, Russia, France, Chicago, Des Moines. Even Disneyland. Nobody says no in Disneyland.

When you think about it, it's quite logical. No government wants to admit its policies are wrong. So the Pentagon sends out the order: Seed the clouds; make it rain; keep the crowds from turning out. But who's going to believe me? I'm just one little guy (five-foot-nine) against the entire United States Government. And look at the weapons the government has: tanks, income tax, television commercials, computers, license-plate bureaus, Ronald Reagan, and the entire Bob Hope Christmas Special. What can I do? That's what I'd like to know.

October 3

I saw an elephant today. A beauty she is. P. T. Barnum would have been proud of her. But she's not for sale.

Tuesday afternoon

Lew Kemp is being followed around by every high school girl in Florida. I don't know what they see in him. He's a few inches taller than I am and he has long blond hair. But looks aren't everything. Right? Personality should count for something. I read the ads all the time. Don't be a schlemiel. Learn to play the glockenspiel or the harmonica. I'll tell you one thing though. I'll never invite him home for a vacation. Never.

Still, I don't care what Lew Kemp does. People without morals don't lead very happy lives, and so I'm going to let him learn the hard way. Besides, I have more important things to think about. I'm going to bomb the Pentagon—not from the ground, but from the air. If governments can bomb individuals from the air, why can't individuals bomb governments? People should have the same rights as governments. People are the government. It's the people who should decide what the government should do, not the other way around. If governments can declare war, so can people. I'm going to be my own army. I'm tired of Peace Marches where nobody comes, and I'm tired of protests where nobody listens. Why are people being paid to manufacture war equipment? Every day people are being paid to manufacture guns and bombs and tanks. And why do the people manufacture such deadly weapons? They get paid to do it, that's why. And why do the people get paid to do it? Because some rich people own the means of production.

When I was growing up, I was told that if I wanted to get something done, I should do it myself. But that's a lie. The most successful people in the world always get others to do things for them. Fight wars for them. Write for them. Kill for them. Even my friend Lew Kemp, since his parents have money all over the place, can hire people to take tests for him. He buys his term papers from some company in Michigan. Me? I'm flunking out because I refuse to go to gym class. Why should I learn to hit a tennis ball or a golf ball? Who am I going to play golf with? The President of General Motors? Fat chance. That's what I want. A sit-in against gym. Who are they to pay some football player $200,000 a year for running up and down a field while people are starving? Where is our sense of values? A specter is haunting Physical Education—the specter of greed. Athletes get all the money, while men like Professor Jelleff work for comparatively nothing. It makes me want to cry. I don't want to declare war, but what choice do I have?

Wednesday morning

I think I should tell you a few things about myself or you're going to get the wrong idea about me. I'm a nice guy, even if I have to say so myself. Still, I refuse to sit back and let my world fall apart just because some people want to pollute the atmosphere, ruin the waterways, and declare war for their private purposes. There comes a time when a man must stand up and be counted, and once I make up my mind to do something, I do it, because that's the kind of guy I am.

Wednesday evening

Once I make up my mind to do something I do it, that's the kind of guy I am, and so I have made up my mind to lead the Revolution myself. I feel it's my duty to kick off the whole thing with a big bang. The Big Bang Theory of Revolution. As Trotsky warned his opponents, "You are unhappy isolated individuals. You are bankrupt. You have played your part. Now you must go where you belong. You are relegated to the dust-heap of history." And there's Trotsky, right on top of the dust-heap. Too bad. A big bang would have helped him a lot. I told Lew about my Big Bang Theory of Revolution, and he became quite excited about it, and there are not many things that excite Lew. After all, he was born with money and that has been a great cushion to his nerves.

"My God! Where did you get an idea like that?" he said.

I told Lew the idea came to me while I was thinking about cloud-seeding. That was hard enough to explain, especially to a guy like Lew Kemp, who is intelligent only when he wants to be. In sixth grade he was the spelling champ of his school, until he missed on the word *hydrophytography,* which refers to the description of water plants. I don't know how they expected a sixth-grader to know that word. It goes to show how the schoolteachers go out of their way to humiliate their students. Humiliation is the common bond of common men, and I must remember that.

Don't get the idea that I'm putting Lew down, because I'm not. I'm anxious to involve Lew in my plan for bombing the Pentagon, because he knows something about flying a plane. Not much, but something. He knows a lot more than I know about it.

Friday afternoon

I walk around the block a couple of times and think about my girl friend, Sally. She's an eighteen-year-old education major at the University of Delaware. I think about that. I also think about white phosphorus. White phosphorus is used to fill hand grenades. White phosphorus is a very difficult thing to think about for a very long time. I've got to get Lew to ask his father for some extra money, money to rent a plane with, money to buy some explosives with.

Monday morning

Today is my lucky day. I have found a magazine article about building an atomic bomb in your basement. What is this world coming to? Why doesn't somebody devise a bomb that won't kill anybody? Maybe a bomb to put an entire country to sleep. I must get my friends to work on that idea.

October 31—early morning

The difficult part about entering an elephant race is to find an elephant that's available. Not only available but fast. Vassar, Yale and the University of Wisconsin are entering elephants in the first National Collegiate Elephant Race, and I think my school should be represented. If I could find an elephant that could outrun Yale, Vassar and Harvard's elephants, it would put my school on the map. I'd be the campus hero. I'd be loved. With Lew Kemp's money and my brains, it shouldn't be too difficult. There used to be small circuses wintering around Sarasota all the time. I think I have a chemistry exam tomorrow.

Tuesday afternoon

Lew is in full agreement with my new philosophy. After hours of discussion, he realizes that we cannot sit back while innocent people die. We need a symbolic act to awaken our country to the ills that beset it, a symbolic act that says the many will not allow their lives to be controlled by the few.

I give him Sir Thomas More's *Utopia* to read, but I know he won't read it. Still, Lew Kemp and I are agreed on one thing: No matter how grand the act, we don't want anyone to get injured, most especially us.

November 1—late morning

I think I'm going to flunk chemistry.

Monday afternoon

Lew Kemp and I are on the way to the Army-Navy Store to see if they have any bombs left over from World War II, though Lew seems to think we'll have to settle for home-made hand grenades.

"More people will sit up and take notice if it's a bomb," I tell him.

"Napalm is good," Lew says, his eyes lighting up. "My father owns a factory in New Jersey, and I bet I could get a secretary to make an order for me."

"Lew, we're not at war with the trees and the grass," I say. "We've got to be subtle. 'Subtlety,' there's the word."

"Hydrophytography. Now there's a word," Lew says, with a touch of bitterness in his voice.

As we enter the store a little brown bell rings behind us. I guess if necessary I'll settle for World War I ammunition, maybe even a cannonball left over from the War between the States. The War Between the States—that's what we call it in the South. We don't call it the Civil War at all. How can war be civil anyway?

A white-haired gentleman wearing an old cap with some medals pinned on it pops up from behind the counter. I am caught off guard by the suddenness of his appearance.

"What can I do for you boys?" he asks. He leans on the glass counter and squints up at me. He doesn't have any teeth.

"We're just looking," I say. Lew has wandered over to the hardware counter and begins fingering some of the tools.

"If you want anything, just holler."

"Thanks." It's then I notice what Lew is doing. He's picking up a hammer and placing it inside his shirt. The old man is at the cash register.

"Do you have any bombs?" I ask, hoping to keep his attention away from Lew. What is Lew up to, anyway? He doesn't have to steal anything. He can buy the whole goddamn store if he wants to.

"What did you say?"

"Do you have any bombs?"

"Bombs?"

"Yeah." I don't know what to do with my hands, so I shove them into my pockets.

"I'm sorry, I don't hear very well. You mean bug bombs? Something to kill bugs with?"

Lew, I can see out of the corner of my eye, has grabbed a fistful of nails and has stuffed them into his blue jeans.

"I want something that will explode," I say quite loudly. If I get hold of Lew, I'm going to explode myself.

"Fireworks?"

"B-O-M-B."

"I can spell," he says.

"But do you have any?" So far he hasn't paid any attention to Lew.

"I'll look."

I walk over to the hardware counter. "What in the hell are you doing?" I whisper to Lew. "Put that stuff back!"

"Mind your own business," Lew says, pressing his elbows close to his sides to keep the hammer in place. I can see the bulge under his shirt. He turns his back on me. Mentally I make a note for my Handbook—*Discipline.*

"You mean something to put flowers in?" the old man asks from the back room. "I think I may have something."

I can see him bending down behind the orange curtain.
"Bomb cases make very nice flower stands."

"You're going to ruin everything," I tell Lew. I've made up my mind to keep him out of the elephant race—that'll show him.

"Get away from me," Lew says.

"No."

"Where's the old guy?"

I don't answer him. Lew's hands go for a yellow screwdriver.

The manager parts the curtain and turns to adjust it on the hooks. "Can I help you with any of that stuff?" he asks Lew.

"No," Lew says. "I'm with him. I'm just looking." He exits hastily through the screen door. Why did I ever bring him along?

I walk toward the manager. What else can I do? "Look, do you think we can order a bomb or two? Could you put in an order for one? I can wait ten days or so."

The old man seizes his cap from his head and tosses it on the floor. "Dammit," he says, "why do you kids come in here making fun of me?"

"I'm not making fun of you," I tell him, trying not to look at his eyes. "I really want a bomb."

"You kids come in here and make fun of me and I won't have it anymore!"

"Look, mister, I'm sorry."

"You're always sorry. Just get going. I don't have to put up with your sky-larking, leastways not around here. I won't have it. You understand?" He has found a broom leaning in the corner, a broom with half its straws missing, and when he tries to herd me to the front of the store his mouth is screwed tight into a pouch.

"I'm not making fun of you," I say. But he refuses to listen. I don't understand why he's so upset all of a sudden. I wasn't making fun of him. I wasn't. It isn't as if there were any other customers in his store. You'd think he'd be happy to get some business, even if all the profits go to the Army and the Navy.

"Get, or I'm calling the cops." For a scarecrow he wields his broom quite effectively, sweeping it in front of him. I guess even the most ordinary of objects can become a weapon.

"All right, all right. I'm going," I tell him.

"You're up to no good, none of you," he says, his wrinkled face turning pale. "You don't want nothing from my store. You just want to waste my time."

"You know something?" I tell him. "I'm really disappointed in your store. Why do you call it an Army-Navy Store if you don't carry their most important items?"

"Get."

"Wars are not fought with brooms you know."

"Get." He slams the screen door in my face with the brown bell rattling away.

Lew is sitting on the curb. A tall man in a checkered shirt enters the Army-Navy Store. He and the old man are probably talking about us right now.

"Give me the stuff," I tell Lew.

"What stuff?"

"You know what stuff. What in the hell did you have to take it for? You want to ruin everything? Suppose we got caught? Then where would our plan be? Right down the drain, along with everything else." The sun is beating down on us, and I'm beginning to sweat. Why don't I get weather like this when there's a Peace March on? I look at Lew sitting there, and I swear I can't figure him out. There he is, dressed in blue jeans and a blue work-shirt, with the middle buttons unbuttoned for easy swindling, and he has one of the best wardrobes in the entire school.

"Well, I didn't get caught, did I?" Lew asks, tying his long blond hair back.

"You didn't get caught? What kind of argument is

that?" I ask him. "You could have gotten caught. That's what matters."

"I could have gotten caught?" Lew stands up to face me. "What kind of argument is that? I *could have* disappeared in a puff of smoke. Don't talk about what could have happened."

I hold out my hand. "Let's not argue," I tell him. "You don't understand argumentation."

"What's your hand out for?"

"Give me the stuff. I'm going to put it back. What's the sense of stealing from the old guy." I glance back over my shoulder and there's the old guy standing behind the plate-glass window, scowling at us, scowling through the reflection of the automobiles that drive by. I hope he hasn't overheard what Lew and I have been talking about.

"You want to declare war on the Pentagon, so start small, I say. He'll never miss the stuff anyway. He doesn't even know what he has in there."

Lew looks at me. I don't know what's going on with him. I really don't. "Come on, Lew," I say. "We don't need that stuff."

"If you go back in there, you'll get caught with it."

"What do you think I am? Stupid?" I look back and the old man has disappeared from the reflections.

Lew hesitates and then his hand goes back inside his shirt. Standing with our backs toward the store, I get from him a hammer, a screwdriver, two electrical cords, a can of car wax, a handful of nails, and a package of cup-hooks. I hadn't even seen him take half the stuff. I put it under my shirt and return to the screen door and peer in. The old man is standing in the back talking with his customer. I can see he has his cap back on.

The bell rings and I walk back inside as nonchalantly as possible.

"Didn't I tell you to get?" the old man says, reaching for his broom.

 "Mister, my friend has cut himself and I need to buy some bandages."

"Take one and get out." The old man points vaguely toward the counter.

"What's the matter, Jed," the man in the checkered shirt says, "these kids giving you trouble again?"

Holding the tools under my shirt, I edge over to the hardware counter and drop them in a bin. They make more noise than I thought they would. "Thanks," I say, hurrying out as quickly as possible, running past the stupid tinkling of the bell.

"Hey!"

"Did you see that? He stole something!"

"Come back here," the old man says.

"It was a hammer or something."

Down the street, the screen-door has slammed again, but Lew and I are running as fast as we can, with Lew running way ahead.

"Thieves! Stop them!"

"Come back here," the man in the checkered shirt is shouting, but I don't know why. Does he really think I'm going to turn around and go back? Even if I told them I was giving the merchandise back, they'd never believe me. I don't want to go to jail. Mentally I make another note for my Handbook for future revolutionaries—*Keep in Shape.* I've been running for only a couple of minutes and already I'm out of breath.

November 8—late afternoon

I have flunked chemistry. But it wasn't my fault. The test was a multiple-choice exam. What kind of chemistry teacher would give a multiple-choice exam? Chemistry should be concerned with the stuff of life, not A, B, C, D or E. Besides, what right does the chemistry teacher have to flunk me? He's probably working at nights on biological weapons.

Maybe he's studying genetics so that he can control my mind and force me to do what I don't want to do. Well, I'll tell you one thing he can't force me to do. He can't force me to study chemistry. I'll show him.

One more thing, and far more important than getting good grades in school. I know somebody who knows somebody who used to work for the Clyde Beatty-Cole Brothers Circus. There may be a chance that they would loan me an elephant. In exchange I would get them publicity so that people will come see their show. Sounds fair enough to me.

Tuesday morning—November 14

I have begun rereading Plato's *Republic* because I am greatly interested in creating the perfect state, a state where everyone will have equal opportunity and will live in harmony. I will set Plato's words at the preface of the Handbook: "But in reality justice was such as we were describing, being concerned, however, not with the outward man, but with the inward, which is the true self and concernment of man: for the just man does not permit the diverse elements within him to interfere with one another, or any of them to do the work of the others—he sets in order his own inner life, and is his own master and his own law, and at peace with himself. . . ."

Trouble begins, however, when a man formulates his own laws, and his own laws run afoul of the laws of his own country. Take the Army, for instance. Who has the right to order another man to kill? Not you. Not me. I would not want such power. Then why do men take such power upon themselves and order my friends away to fight and to die.

Which brings me to my older brother, Sam. Samuel Ellsworth Wainwright, whose initials spelled SEW; hence he hated to have his initials on anything. As soon as he could, he ran off and joined the Army and was sent to Vietnam. Not sent exactly. He wanted to go. He wanted to see what it was like firsthand. I don't even know how much he got to see. He had hardly stepped off the plane when we got the telegram that said—well, you know what it said. How can a man be at peace with himself when his country is continually at war?

I don't want to think about the perfect state anymore. It depresses me. Maybe my fifth-grade teacher was right. "Pessimist" is the word for me.

November 16—early morning

The Clyde Beatty-Cole Brothers elephant is pregnant, so the circus doesn't want her to race. I guess that sounds reasonable. But now everybody is counting on me. There is quite a bit of talk about us entering the elephant race and beating out the Ivy League schools. I don't know how I get involved in these things. I think I'm an over-achiever.

Tuesday morning—November 21

I have recovered from my depression long enough to send a special-delivery letter to Herdie Naismith of the University of Delaware, along with a money order for $300. The $300 comes from the generosity of Elias Kemp, Lew's father, though of course Mr. Kemp has no idea to what good purposes his money is being put. But what difference does it make where the money comes from? A revolutionary cannot take the time to go into banking. It would positively destroy the purity of his purpose.

Of course, I have enough money so that I could have called Herdie long distance to explain everything, but neither Lew nor myself trust the phone company. Phones all over the place are being tapped. And even if the phone is not tapped, there is always the possibility that some patriotic operator would overhear our conversation. It is for these reasons that I have given express orders to Herdie that he is not to call me while I'm home on vacation. No matter how excited he is.

Thanksgiving

Herdie called. Some people just don't understand a thing. Someone once said that disaster in the world is caused by two kinds of people: those who can't follow orders and those who can *only* follow orders. Herdie can't follow orders, can't follow a simple instruction, and now he has ruined everything.

He wanted to know what kind of bomb I wanted, how much it should weigh, whether he should use TNT or Amatol. I hardly pick up the phone and he's bombarding me with these questions, and I have very little idea what he's talking about.

All of this going on over the phone, and my parents are sitting in front of the television set, not more than ten or twelve feet away. My father is falling asleep, wavering under a newspaper, but my mother is watching my every move. I must look suspicious even in my own house.

"We have a lot to be thankful for, Jon," she says, shaking my father's arm, but he doesn't respond. He grunts slightly and shifts his weight.

"Do you want anything more to eat?" my mother asks me, but I shake my head.

"Stop feeding him," my father says. Then he rolls over. "He's too fat now. Why are you always feeding him?"

My mother's still looking at me, so I stretch the phone cord as far away from the living room as possible. "I don't think he's fat," she says.

"Hello, hello," Herdie's yelling into the phone. How can a guy like Herdie, who is supposed to be so intelligent, be so stupid? True, I could have hung up on him, but that might have angered Herdie, causing unnecessary delays. The delays will make a psychological wreck out of me. I can't wait forever.

Besides, a true Revolutionary must be a gambler. (I must save that sentence for the Handbook, to go with the quote from Plato. A page or two of aphorisms will attract a wider readership.)

In addition, the telephone, in spite of its obvious dangers, must be the third arm of the third world. Large Brutus-Cassius-type meetings must be avoided. That's the advantage of having codes and code names to cover the operation, so that conversations can be held in the middle of a living room within hearing distance of one's parents.

I must confess, though, that I am quite proud of myself over how cleverly I handled Herdie's phone call. I threw in all sorts of false information, just in case anyone was listening —either a telephone operator, or my parents, or a CIA man somewhere. The gist of my ruse was that there is a science fair being held at school and that one of the main exhibits is going to be a demonstration of explosives. I tried to disguise my voice by talking deeper than usual, but that only confused Herdie, so I told him to hang up. I'll call him tomorrow.

November 24—late morning

I just read in the paper that the zoo in Sanford, Florida, has acquired an Indian elephant. My problem now is whether I should simply ask the zoo officials if I can borrow it or whether I should just go up there at night and take it. If I ask them and they say no, then when the elephant is missing, they will immediately know who's guilty. Though, if they would lend it to me, it would make my life much more simple. The entire school is counting on me to beat Vassar and Yale, but I bet the kids from Vassar and Yale can just go out and buy an elephant. Can a used elephant beat a new one?

It's a good feeling, though, to have the girls look up to me. Every once in a while a girl will approach me and ask me if I'm the one who is going to represent our school in the elephant race. How can I have the heart to say no?

Friday evening

In the phone booth. A revolutionary is a man who says *no,* but how can I say no to Herdie when I'm not at all sure what I'm talking about. Bombs come in many different shapes and sizes. It's not as if all bombs are alike. Bombs are made for many different and specific purposes, and so I am confused about what to ask for. Lew and I agreed the bomb should be lightweight, since I am going to carry it on the plane myself. I can't exactly call upon a crew of men to load the weapon on the plane for me. Also the bomb should go off on impact, and the impact should be such that, although we do not hurt anybody, it is apparent to the world at large that I and my friends, I and my brothers, mean business. As far as I am concerned this attack on the Pentagon should go down in the books, right along with Pearl Harbor and the Bay of Pigs.

That's the way it stands, and after much back-and-forth discussion (my arm is wearing out dropping quarters into the phone) Herdie convinces me that an incendiary bomb filled with something called Thermite should do the trick.

"You can also have a blockbuster bomb, if you want," Herdie says. Herdie is quite excited about the project, but I don't know whether he shares my revolutionary fervor or simply enjoys the idea of getting paid. I'm always amazed to find out how much people are paid to create things to destroy people.

"A blockbuster? What's that?"

"It was used in World War II a couple of times. The English had something called a giant blockbuster."

"That explains it perfectly."

"But there's a problem with them. The case is so thin that they have to be dropped by parachute to keep them from breaking on the way down."

"So why bring it up?"

"Because I think the blockbuster is what you want. It makes a tremendous noise and has very little penetrating power. That means it's a safe kind of bomb."

"Lots of noise though."

"Lots of noise."

I think about that for a few seconds. Since I'm paying good money for this long-distance call, I don't want to think about it for too long. "Ok," I tell him. "It sounds OK to me. After all I don't want to murder anyone. It's just a symbolic thing."

"Most bombs are," Herdie says.

"The one that killed my brother wasn't very symbolic," I shoot back at him.

Herdie remains in an embarrassed silence. I feel sorry for what I said. I didn't mean to embarrass him.

Herdie clears his throat. "Look," he says at last, "if you want symbolism, why don't you use a leaflet bomb. We could write up something that would really shock everybody. Just stuff a bomb with leaflets and cover Washington with our message."

"What would we say?"

"I don't know. But you and Lew could think of something. MAKE LOVE NOT WAR. BRING THE BOYS HOME."

"Forget it. I'm not in the printing business," I tell him. I'm also tired of slogans. Slogans go in one ear and out the other."

"OK. An incendiary bomb and a blockbuster."

"Check. And look, Herdie, if one word of this leaks out to anybody, to anybody, you'll be the one who is dropped from the plane."

"Hey, man, don't get tough. I'm your friend. Remember?"

"Some friend. I tell you not to call me under any circumstances, and you call me while my parents are sitting right there in the living room. What do you think I do, go home and announce—Well, Mom and Dad, I'm going to declare war on the Pentagon today?"

"You said to call you," Herdie protests.

"I did not." If there's one thing I know it's when a man is not telling the truth. It is going to be difficult to run the organization if my fellow-members have no devotion to the truth.

"Wait a minute. I have the letter right here in my back pocket."

I deposit several more quarters into the telephone, and listen as Herdie unfolds a piece of paper. How do I know if that's my letter or not?

"Here it is," Herdie says. "No matter how you feel, you are to call me."

"Are you sure?"

"That's what you wrote. Don't you know what you wrote?"

"I left out the word 'not'?"

"There's no 'not' here."

"You should have known that I meant to say *not* to call me. Why would I want you to call me?"

"I'm not a mind reader," Herdie insists.

"All right, forget about it. Just see that it doesn't happen again."

"Check."

"And I don't want you mention this to anybody. Even if you see Sally. Remember, nobody is to know a thing.

"Don't worry about it, man. If anybody's going to make a mistake, it's going to be you."

"I meant to write do *not* call me," I tell him, and on those words, Herdie hangs up.

Memo for the Handbook: a chapter on traitors and how to deal with them.

Memo for the Handbook: Secretaries cannot belong exclusively to businessmen and corporate executives. Revolutionaries also need secretaries. Someone who can be trusted to proofread instructions and all letters to members of the organization. Organization is the key—even for anarchy. Most especially for anarchy.

November 28—afternoon

I cannot make up my mind about the Sanford Zoo. I do not think it is my fault, because I believe that it is very easy to be wishy-washy about an elephant. An elephant is so huge that a single mind cannot encompass it all. I could ask Lew Kemp to ask his father if he knows somebody who has an elephant, but if Lew Kemp gets involved, he will want to race the elephant himself. Then where will I be? What is the use of a great idea if one does not have the means to execute it?

When I was six or seven years old I had the great idea of turning my bicycle into an airplane by attaching a motor and cardboard wings. I worked a long time on the project and all I wanted to do was drive it off the roof to test it. But my parents would not allow it. Not on your life. They kept telling me I would break a leg or get hurt or even kill myself. I showed them sketches of an airplane made by Leonardo da Vinci, but they pointed out that since Leonardo had already tried it, why should I? But that doesn't strike me as a good argument now. It's hard to think of something Leonardo didn't try, though I may come up with something yet.

Wednesday

Running a revolution can cause a lot of headaches. Lew has suggested that we have a troop of persons on the ground, hundreds of people armed with Molotov cocktails, but I'm against it. That can lead to serious repercussions. Also, if too many people get involved, the plan will surely leak out. In any group of twelve people or more, at least one is going to be an FBI man. No matter how serious or high-minded, at least one will turn out to be a traitor. In class, for example, when I was in third grade, whenever the teacher left the room she always designated someone to write down the names of people who talked. If anyone even so much as whispered, their names would end up on a list. The only trouble was that I was always the one chosen to take down the names. I was chosen to betray my friends. I was the one who could determine who would be punished and who wouldn't, who would have extra homework and who wouldn't. And I did it!

After fourth grade, however, I refused to be the name-taker or the monitor. I had learned my lesson. The fourth grade was the turning point in my life. I had a choice. To remain faithful to the duty and responsibilities which had been thrust upon me or to be beaten up, and since I did not and do not like the sight of blood, I often erased the culprit's name. Discipline was the teacher's job—not mine.

All of which leads me to the conclusion that there must be an ideal size for a revolutionary organization. Two, I think. When more than two people get involved in a project, trouble is certain to break out.

Thursday morning

Sometimes I think that if more than one person gets involved, problems will break out.

December 1—evening

Our school newspaper has announced that a fraternity at the University of California has decided to enter the elephant race against Yale, Harvard, Vassar and me. I think I have problems! Imagine trying to ship an elephant all the way across the United States! I wonder what it would cost to mail it.

December 8

The French Club has volunteered to design a blanket with our school colors on it, a blanket that the elephant can wear in the race. A warmup jacket. But what I want to know is, where are the other schools getting their elephants from? There must be a mail-order house somewhere.

The more I think about it, and I think about it through all my classes, the more I begin to realize that stealing an elephant is a bit impractical. The penalties might be pretty stiff, and the rewards don't seem all that great to me. Perhaps I better call the whole thing off. But how will I live with the disgrace? What would Sir Thomas More do?

Tuesday

I need to assign a pickup point for the bombs. And I still need to find a plane. Winning the elephant race will be easy compared to this one. Possibility. We could, if we wished to save money, drive from the university to the District of Columbia and rent a plane near the Pentagon itself.

Hangup. Hiring a plane near the Pentagon will make it easier for the FBI to trace it later.

Flying all the way from Florida to Washington is out of the question, for somewhere in the back of my mind lurks the suspicion that I am susceptible to air-sickness.

Another possibility. Lew suggests that we might be able to get a private plane from his father's company. This is good because it is the same plane Lew has taken a lesson or two in. Familiarity breeds acquaintance. On the other hand, borrowing a plane from Lew's father will put us at the mercy of the company. We could use the plane only when it would be convenient for the company. Suppose Lew and I devised a lot of elaborate plans and at the last minute the company decided to use its plane, thus depriving us of it. Then where would we be? Standing around with a couple of bombs. That would make for a good conversation-opener. Also, if anything happens to the plane, there would be a direct line to Lew's father. And Lew is not a very big distance from his father. Neither am I for that matter.

No, I do not desire to place myself at the mercy of capitalist dogs. Nor do I desire to be imprisoned. The only reasonable alternative, it seems to me, is to find a home base and stick with it. Before a man can do anything correctly he needs a base of operation.

Thursday noon

Sally keeps calling me, asking why I don't write to her and why I don't come up for a weekend. But she has to realize that revolutionaries have no time for frivolities. She says she has only one life to lead and she wants to enjoy it while she can. I tell her we have only one world to live in and we'd better make it a good one. She's angry, but if she wants to find somebody else, let her. She'll soon find out how dull her other boyfriends are by comparison. Besides, I need a liberated woman.

Thursday night

To prepare myself for the ordeals that lie ahead, I decided to spend a couple of hours rereading James Bond. What I need, I now realize, is my own private air force, such as is found in *Goldfinger.* Unfortunately, for a student of my limited means, a private air force is out of the question. Someone has to pay the pilots. Someone has to buy the planes. Someone has to keep everything in good repair. I guess that's why I like James Bond so much. He never worries about those things. A new note for the Handbook: Revolutionaries will go only to documentary movies. No *Hot Rock.* No *Dracula.* No *Singing in the Rain.* And absolutely no Doris Day. Maybe to James Bond films though, because you can pick up some valuable tips on espionage and spying.

I could write to Castro and ask if he might lend me a plane. I'm sure he can't be very fond of the Pentagon. But he probably wouldn't read my letter. Even if he did read it, he would think I am some kind of crackpot. Besides, my Spanish is lousy. When I took Spanish in high school, I almost flunked the course.

The hard, cold facts of running a revolution are much different from the side most people see.

December 15

When I was six years old, I had a Flash Gordon disintegrating-ray gun. I could use something like that now. I'd point the gun at the elephant in the Sanford Zoo, cause it to disintegrate, and then reassemble it back at my school. Why don't Vassar and Yale and the University of Wisconsin hold a horse race instead? A horse I can get with a snap of my finger.

Saturday

It is the ruling class that has the power to make its ideas felt, for the rulers control or have access to television, radio, newspapers and magazines. It is possible to start your own magazine, but nobody will distribute it. Also it costs a lot of money to disseminate ideas, to circulate manifestos, to publish magazines. I had a friend in high school who published an underground newspaper. It was full of good ideas on how to improve the educational system. What was the result of his effort? He was expelled. Freedom of speech? Show me a person in public school with freedom of speech.

I believe I shall use the above paragraph for the preface to my Revolutionary's Handbook.

December 18—evening

I don't want to cheat, but I am beginning to doubt my powers. Some people are just not cut out to be elephant thieves. Perhaps I could rent an elephant costume and dress up some of my friends. I know a couple of people who would be quite good at pretending to be an elephant. It's too bad my parents didn't have enough money to send me to Yale or Harvard; then getting an elephant would be no problem at all.

According to the rules of the Great Elephant Race, I must submit a photograph by January 1 or else I will be disqualified. I don't know why they insist upon a photograph. Is ABC's "Wide World of Sports" televising the event? I'll show them. I'll get an elephant into that race if I have to buy one.

Tuesday

After reading the papers about planes being hijacked to Cuba, Israel, Rome, and to almost everywhere else, it occurs to me that Lew and I might hijack a plane to Washington, D.C. Telling a Northeast Yellow Bird to change its course from New York to the Pentagon has it special charms. Even the Goodyear Blimp is up for grabs. No end to alternatives. And that's the problem. Too many choices. I am about to abandon the project out of despair, for choice is what creates human lives, but wrecks revolutions. In a revolution, the choice must be narrowed in the right direction so that people will choose to follow, will choose to go along with the changes.

No, that doesn't make sense either. What I want to do, beyond choice, is to free myself, my friends, and millions of young men everywhere from the chains of a corrupt military establishment. Is that so very much to ask?

December 20

I have taken a photograph of the elephant in the Sanford Zoo and have sent that photograph off to the Great Elephant Race. What difference can it possibly make?

December 22

The Monroe Doctrine of Human Relationships: Beware of entangling alliances. Christmas is a good time to push the doctrine into action, for everywhere people are trying to give and take without hurting someone's feelings. Victims caught in the toils of materialism, a materialism without a dialectic. My solution is not to buy anybody anything and simply strive for purity of spirit. Except my parents, of course. I have to buy my parents something. And maybe something for Lew because he usually gives me something expensive. I know Sally expects something, and Herdie is doing so much work for me up in Delaware that I should at least send him a book, some little present to promote the spirit of Brotherhood. And I'll send Professor Jelleff a card. But aside from those people, nothing. I have to save my money for the important things.

Perhaps I should send a card to the officials of the Sanford Zoo just to soften them up.

December 24

I'm home. It's too bad I live so close to school, otherwise it would seem more like a vacation. The palm trees are swaying on the lawn and my mother has a Christmas tree blinking in the front window. There's really no end to the confusion, if you let yourself think about it.

December 25—evening

Sally called tonight. She said to have a good Christmas, even though she is very angry with me for not inviting her down. When she gets my present, she'll feel better. I'd better mail it tomorrow, special delivery.

December 26

My present from Lew arrived! It's a round-trip plane ticket to Washington, D.C., where he will meet me. We'll make arrangements for hiring the plane and then we'll go to New Jersey to spend a few days with his parents before returning to school. My parents are quite upset about my leaving so soon. My father says the last time he was in Washington there was nothing to do and there's still nothing to do as far as he can tell. My mother wants to know what Lew's mother is like and why Lew can't come here. She says I should stay until New Year's at least, but she doesn't understand what's going on. I really don't think I can take the pressure anymore.

December 27

A long talk with Lew. I've convinced him that we should get our hair cut. Most likely it will make it easier to talk with the man who owns the plane. Disguises are another good idea.

I've also convinced Lew that we should wear business suits so we look like typical businessmen, whatever typical businessmen look like. The suits, coupled with short hair, will help us to make a good impression. I'm going to borrow a suit from a friend of mine (it is necessary to economize. From those who have to those who need—that's how the motto goes), but Lew refuses to wear borrowed clothes. He says that he has never worn borrowed clothes in his life and he has no intention of starting now.

Somehow I can't trust the revolutionary zeal of a person who refuses to wear borrowed clothes, though I know Lew has stuck through everything so far. Lew laid out $500 for the Peace March and $300 for the bombs, and now we have to pay for the plane. The high cost of things is part of the Capitalist Plot to destroy revolutionary movements. My Handbook is going to make that perfectly clear. Hard, cold, concrete facts about budgetary matters must be spelled out in black and white.

If people think the cost of a revolution shouldn't be taken into consideration, they have another think coming. Revolutions aren't games. They're big business like everything else.

December 29—A.M.

Lew and I are on the way to a private airport where we'll make our contact. This is tricky business and Lew and I have to be particularly careful not to give ourselves away. Rule Number One: Plan everything ahead.

December 29—noon

Haircut. Check. Shoes shined. Check. Pants pressed. Check. The pants are almost as shiny as my shoes, but beggars can't be choosers. If a friend is going to lend you his clothes, you can't expect him to lend you his best clothes. The suit I have on doesn't really fit me correctly because my friend is slightly taller than I am. I don't know why all my friends are so tall, though I'm sure it's not their fault. There's no law that says everyone has to be the same size. Not yet anyway. Perhaps Lew's attitude toward borrowed clothes is the correct one.

Fingernails clean. They'll have to do. Mustache and dark glasses in place. Check.

Lew and I are dressed to kill—though I don't mean that quite as literally as it sounds.

December 29—2 P.M.

What I'm thinking is that we might not have to hire a plane. Maybe the American Civil Liberties Union would lend us one for a couple of hours. Maybe I can get a combination deal, a private plane and a skywriter all in one. Perhaps for the same price. With a skywriter people could not possibly mistake our motives. I wonder if they charge by the word the way Western Union does. If we could afford it, I'd have the pilot spell out "hydrophytography" for Lew's sake. Lew would get a big kick out of that.

THE GENERAL GOOD NOT GENERAL MOTORS.

When it comes to slogans, a revolutionary might well look to Madison Avenue. Why not? Those guys can sell everything, even rat poison. It doesn't make any difference to them.

December 29—5:30 P.M.

When Lew and I arrive at the airport, a great hulk of a man ambles over to us. He must be six-foot-five, dressed in khaki pants, a T-shirt and a light jacket, everything covered with grease. He's a big guy all right and he doesn't seem to be bothered by the cold. I look at him and I've never seen so many muscles on one man. He must lift the planes off the ground, not fly them. Right away I don't think he's the man for the job. I'm actually hoping for a pilot smaller than I am. Someone I can handle should the going get rough. Maybe someone who is slightly anemic. I actually want somebody competent, but pliable. Very pliable. The hulk brushes some dirt from his T-shirt and pushes his goggles back. Running his stubby fingers through his crewcut, he leaves a light film of grease on his hair. His fingernails aren't as clean as ours.

"Are you Slade Klusewzki?" Lew asks.

"Yeah, that's right. You guys friends of my nephew?"

"No . . ."

"Yeah," Lew interrupts. "That's right."

"How's Jack doing?"

"Fine, fine. He sends his best."

"Good kid."

"Yeah, really fine. Everybody likes him a lot."

"Fine boy."

"Yeah."

That brings the conversation to a standstill for a while, until Slade looks at me. He offers me a stick of gum. I wave it away. "Well, you guys interested in my plane?" he asks. His voice reminds me not so much of a human voice as the sound of a train rumbling in a tunnel.

"Well, Mr. Klusewzki," I say.

"Call me Slade."

"OK. I'm Howie Smith and this is Jack Jones," I say, indicating Lew, just so Lew understands who he is. Slade is covered with grease, so we don't shake hands. I like Slade well enough. He seems friendly. At least that's my first impression of him.

"We'd like a plane for February 26," I say right out. There doesn't seem to be any sense in beating around the bush. I try to talk quickly because I'm not used to a mustache on my lip. I've given up trying to disguise my voice because it takes too much concentration. I have nothing but admiration for those ventriloquists who can walk on stage and throw their voices all over the place. I wish I could do that. That would be a useful talent for a revolutionary.

"Either one of you guys fly?" Slade asks. He opens a pocket on his pants and pulls out out a pack of cigarettes. He offers us a smoke, but when Lew reaches for one, I catch his hand.

"No thanks. We don't smoke," I tell him. Lew, slightly confused, drops his hand in a careless gesture.

"That's good. It's too late for me to stop. I tried to substitute chewing gum, but it's not the same thing. I take a couple of chews and the flavor's gone." He spits his gum to the ground and lights a cigarette instead.

"We don't fly," I tell him, trying to keep the conversation to the point. If you don't keep your plan in front of you at all times, it gets lost in the confusion.

"I've had a couple of lessons," Lew says, but I kick him lightly in the ankle to keep him from volunteering unnecessary information. "But I don't have a license," he adds, glaring in my direction.

"That's all right because nobody goes up in Winnie Mae without me. It's my plane, so I do the flying. Too many people think they should be pilots, but they have no business driving a car, let alone an airplane." Slade drags on his Camel and blows the smoke out in circles, circles within circles. "Not many guys can blow circles like that," he says.

I agree with him. Watching Slade blow cigarette rings has a tranquilizing effect on me.

"So what do you guys want to go up for?"

"You see my friend here," I say, indicating Lew. "He's in the United States for the first time and . . ."

"Oh, a foreigner," he says, but he says it friendly enough. "Where are you from?"

"He's from Japan," I answer quickly.

"He don't look like no Japanese to me."

"His parents are American. He just hasn't been in America too long."

"So why does he go around in dark glasses. Can't see anything with dark glasses on."

"The light hurts his eyes," I explain.

"Then how does he hope to pilot a plane?"

"I don't," Lew says. "I just said I had a few lessons."

I remove my sunglasses just to be hospitable. "His father was a marine and his mother's from the Philippines. This is his first few months in the United States, so I thought it would be nice if I could show my friend our country's capital from the air."

Slade removes an oily rag from his back pocket and wipes his face with it. "Oh. You mean he wants to see the Washington Monument and places like that?" From his posture, Slade reminds me of a wrestler I once knew.

"Yeah. And the Pentagon," Lew adds, trying to be casual about the whole thing.

"I'm not very good at giving guided tours, if you know what I mean," Slade says apologetically. "But I'll do the best I can."

"The Washington Monument is one of the first things I want to see," Lew says, trying to correct himself.

"Yeah, you guys are OK," Slade remarks off-handedly. "Whatja say your names were?"

"Howie Smith and I'm Jack Jones."

Slade looks at me quizzically. "I thought you said you were Howie Smith," he says, indicating me.

"No, he's Howie Smith," I say.

"I'm sorry. I'm just not very good at names," he says.

"Me either."

"I'm Slade."

"I know that." My mind is racing, trying to think of some way to change the subject. "You know. I just don't think you can get the feel of Washington on the ground. You've got to see it from the air. Then you get to see just how well the place is laid out. We thought that the best way to see it would be from the air."

"Yeah. I'd like to see it from the air," Lew adds, trying to give me moral support.

Slade blows his nose into an oily rag. "Well, me and Winnie Mae usually get quite a few calls, so I have to be particular who I take up." He stares at the rag a moment and then stuffs it into his pocket. It's a habit everybody has, I guess. Blowing your nose, and then staring at the handkerchief to see what's there. "Now that the weather is getting warmer, business is starting to pick up, if you know what I mean."

Lew and I don't say anything, but I nod my head in agreement. I nod it weakly.

"But you two look OK to me," Slade continues. "February 26 you say? That's a long way off. But that's OK, I guess. What time do you want to go up?"

I look at Lew and he looks at me. We haven't really discussed the time. Now, this is where prior experience really comes in handy. If we go up too early, it will leave the rest of the day for the people to begin investigation. We can't go up at night because our attack will lose its impact then. There have to be people around to ensure the best reaction.

"I don't know. When is it best for you?" I ask.

"How long do you want the plane for? An hour? Two hours?"

That's another thing Lew and I haven't discussed. We have to allow enough time so we can maneuver Slade over the Pentagon without getting him too suspicious.

"How about three hours?"

"Three hours? That's a long time. It won't take you that long to see the sights."

"I want to take my time," Lew says. "I don't want to be rushed."

"Well, believe me, an hour, an hour and a half is plenty. I'll tell you what. Why don't you see how you feel when you get up there. We'll go up about ten o'clock or so, and then I'll have plenty of time to get back for lunch. How does that sound to you?"

"I guess that's all right." I glance at Lew, but he doesn't say anything.

"What's the weather going to be like?" Lew asks.

"Too early to tell yet, but we've been having a good winter."

"Yeah. The weather has been pretty good lately," I agree. I figure the more I agree with him, the better he will like me. That's the way people are. The more you agree with them, the more they like you, and the weather is one of the easiest things in the world to agree about.

"What about your eyes?" Slade asks Lew. "If the sun's too bright, won't it hurt your eyes?" Slade seems quite concerned. "Maybe it will be better if we go up in the evening. Say, at twilight. Then the light won't be so bright. It can be quite bright up there. Especially with the sun bouncing off the tops of the buildings. Maybe twilight will be best. It makes no difference to me. I work all the time anyway."

Lew points to his glasses. "Special glasses," he says. "I'll be all right."

"I can't be responsible."

"We know that," I agree.

"It's just today," Lew adds. "It only happens every once in a while."

"I heard about a guy who was blind during the day but who could see at night. You aren't one of those kind of guys are you?"

"No."

"You've taken flying lessons, you say?"

"Just a few."

"I think the morning will be all right," I say. "How much do you charge?" There is a time to be practical.

"Twenty bucks."

"For the morning?"

"An hour."

"Oh, an hour." Lew shrugs his shoulders. What's money to him?

"That'll be OK," I answer. Why did Lew have to pick such an expensive plane? I bet it's a habit he learned from his father.

"Once you get up there, you'll love it," Slade says.

"Nothing like it," Lew agrees.

"Nothing like it in the whole world. You have the whole city at your feet like you were the king. The first time I ever went up in a plane it changed my whole life," Slade says, crushing his cigarette. "I didn't want to come down."

This flight is going to change my whole life too, but I don't say anything.

"Where's the plane?" Lew asks. When it comes to matters like this, he is much more practical than I am.

"It's in the hangar. Come on, I'll show it to you. I'm as proud of Winnie Mae as I am of my wife and kids."

I think to myself—abolition of private property, but I don't say anything. Instead I follow Lew and Slade across the airfield. I have to know the layout of the place because it is from this place that we are going to make our escape when the plane lands. Slade is such a big guy that handling him is going to be a bit touchy. He seems like a nice guy too. I hate to get him involved in this, but what choice do I have?

"Ever hear of Clyde Klusewzki?"

"No," Lew says.

"I guess you wouldn't because you haven't been in the country for too long, but he used to be a ballplayer. Third baseman for the Chicago White Sox. He's a member of my family. A distant relative of mine. I used to watch him all the time. It's a big difference when it's somebody you know. You get more involved in the game. I only met him once though. You like baseball?"

"I really don't know too much about it," Lew says.

In the hangar is an old yellow and blue monstrosity that Slade refers to as his plane. The sight of it so unnerves Lew that he removes his glasses and walks slowly around it.

"Are you sure the Smithsonian Institution isn't looking for this?" he asks.

Slade pats the tail of the plane. "This here is my very own 1933 Lockheed Winnie Mae. They don't make planes like this anymore. Take us anywhere we want to go and back again. That's why I charge a little more than the other guys, I have something special to offer. I have plane buffs from all over the United States who want to take a ride in it. In fact there's a guy from Rhinebeck, New York, who wants to buy the thing, but I'm not going to part with my Winnie Mae. It's like a marriage. Till death do us part."

"1933?" I ask.

"How old are you? Eighteen, nineteen?"

"Eighteen."

"Well, it's long before your time."

Sometimes I get the feeling that everything was long before my time. I walk around the plane and look toward Lew for help. How safe can this plane be? I can't afford to crash with a couple of bombs on me. If I were pressed, I'd have to admit that I am more distressed by the yellow and blue combination than I am by the state of the plane.

Slade opens the door of the cabin and spills some dirty laundry off the front seat. A couple of pairs of white sweat-socks and a yellow shirt crumbled into a ball. He tosses them to the ground. "This plane is a real pearl," he says. "Same kind used by Wiley Post when he flew around the world."

"Wiley Post?"

"Yeah, died in a plane crash with Will Rogers. You heard of him I hope."

"I heard of Will Rogers, but not of the other guy." Plane crash, I think. That gives me a lot of hope. Maybe all those religious fanatics are right. If man was meant to fly, God would have created humans with wings.

I think Slade senses a certain nervousness on our part, because he begins to calm us down. "Hell, you two have nothing to worry about. I shouldn't have even mentioned nothing about Post. That's me and my big mouth again. But, look, I've been flying this plane for a long time now. Me and Winnie Mae have seen a lot of miles together."

"We'll meet you February 26," I say, trying to cut him

short. I am in no mood to hear his travelogue. What does it matter where he's been. I just want to get everything set.

Slade picks the laundry up from the mud. "You want to put fifteen down so I'll be sure you'll be here?" he asks. "Just a token of good faith. It's a pain when people say they want you and then decide not to show up at the last minute."

"We'll be here. That's one thing you can count on," I tell him. "Death, taxes, and the fact that we'll be here on February 26."

Lew pulls out his wallet and counts out a ten and a five. Every revolutionary organization should have a man like Lew around.

On our way home I can tell that Lew isn't very happy about Winnie Mae, but the way I look at it is that it's a plane. It'll do. We can't expect to charter a private jet, because that will make it almost impossible to drop the load. "Christ," Lew says over and over, "I'm not going up in that thing sober." I can tell that I'm going to have trouble with him, but at least we're set. The next thing I'm going to do is buy a revolver. Lew is going to go up in that plane whether he likes it or not. We've gone to too much trouble to turn back now.

Did Che have such troubles with his cohorts? Did Mao? Did Lady Godiva? Now, there's a symbolic act for you. Riding naked through the city streets to protest against taxes. That's the kind of protest I'd like to see more of.

January 3

We're back in contact with Herdie. He's finally returned from his vacation and things are picking up. Everything is nearly completed at his end, though I don't understand what's taking him so long. Why didn't he work through Christmas like the rest of us? In the future I want factory workers, men and women who know how to punch a time-clock, people who can get the work done on time. Maybe

 I should transfer to a university up north so I can be closer to the Establishment. Then I could strike quickly.

January 5

I have taken a collection from the people at school. I now have a couple of hundred dollars to take care of feeding and transporting the elephant. Once I get the elephant, though, I'll have to house it somewhere until the time of the race. I can't keep it in my room.

I may be only a freshman at college, but I've learned some things. One thing I've learned is that my parents pay hundreds of dollars just to rent a bed for me to sleep in. The college owns the room, so I have no rights. No rights at all. Why can't I keep an elephant? If my roommate doesn't object, and if the elephant doesn't interfere with my studies, why should the administration mind? It can't hurt anything. In fact, an elephant might improve my studies, opening up whole new avenues of thought. I definitely need stimulus from somewhere.

Sunday night—late

Very late. I have awakened from my sleep, awakened by a dream. I usually don't remember my dreams, but this dream I remember. In my dream I'm being carried off by a great bald eagle. The eagle appears as huge as an elephant. A huge eagle carrying me over the mountains of Korea.

"Don't drop me in Korea," I say, speaking very calmly, considering the situation I'm in.

"That's all right," the eagle says. In dreams animals talk and no one considers it unusual at all. "If I drop you, you'll be safe. There are plenty of Americans here."

Then we fly over Vietnam. "Don't worry," says the eagle. "If I drop you here, you'll be safe. There are plenty of Americans in Vietnam."

And then we are over Cuba. "That's all right," says the eagle. "There's still an American base in Cuba."

When I wake up, I'm on the floor of my bedroom.

January 11

Montgomery Frankel, a black sophomore majoring in Business Administration, has agreed to come along with me on the elephant project. I don't think he's as temperamental as Lew, and as a business major, he can give me cold hard facts about the economics of the situation. He also claims he can get his hands on a truck, a large one he can drive, and I think that is a lot to say in his favor, for I have to get the elephant to North Carolina somehow. Montie and I have been up all night discussing the problems, and the problems seem to be getting out of hand, but we will press forward. The consensus is that for $250 we can bribe the guard at the Sanford Zoo, convincing him to downplay the disappearance of an elephant for a couple of days. It's a risk, but no great accomplishments occur without risk. Montie will drive to Sanford tomorrow and give it a try. I wonder if there is a law against bribing a zoo-keeper?

At least one good thing has emerged from all this. Lew and Montie are really on my side. They look up to me and believe in me. Without friends I would be nowhere.

January 12—very late

The plan has been fixed. After the elephant race, Montie will drive our elephant back to the Sanford Zoo and I will join Lew at his parents' house in New Jersey where we will rest up and attend to last-minute details, although I hope there won't be any. Then on February 25, Lew and I will take a bus to Wilmington, Delaware. The bombs will be waiting for us in a locker at the Wilmington bus station. Herdie is supposed to mail us the locker key by air-mail special delivery, so I should have the key in my hand very soon. Good old Herdie. He's been working around the clock to get the bombs ready. He must be exhausted. Actually, Lew and I aren't feeling so hot ourselves.

January 16

The zoo-keeper, for a modest $300, has decided to loan us the elephant. Since the elephant race is to be held in Chapel Hill, North Carolina, at the University of North Carolina football field on February 8, we will be allowed to pick up the elephant on February 5 at three o'clock in the morning. If anything happens to the elephant, however, it will be my responsibility. In order to protect himself, the zoo-keeper will report the theft of the elephant to the proper authorities on February 7.

I don't like the arrangements very much, but what choice do I have?

Monday

Is it possible to open the window of a plane while it is in flight? Will the air pressure be lowered so much that Lew and I will be sucked out of the plane the way it happens in *Goldfinger?* Why don't I know anything? What have I done with my life? There ought to be a school for revolutionaries to teach them such things.

January 23

If anything happens to me on this assignment, I hope I don't have to go to the hospital. Hospitals are deadlier than bombs. When I was twelve, for example, my father had a stroke and was rushed to St. Mary's. I had permission to leave school and I hopped on my bicycle and pedaled as fast as I could. I think I was crying but I don't remember. Everything was blurry. I don't think I ever rode a bike so fast in my life, and by the time I reached the hospital, my yellow T-shirt was drenched with sweat.

As I arrived in the parking lot, I saw my brother, Sam, hitting his fist against the hood of our car, with my mother trying to calm him down. My brother told me that the hospital had kept my father on a stretcher out in the corridor and wouldn't admit him until she could prove that we could pay the bill. That's what's wrong with this country, indifference to human suffering. Money over people. That's what I'm out to correct.

Sam borrowed my bicycle and rode around for a while and that calmed him down a bit. I had never seen Sam as angry as that.

Thursday

What Lew and I really need is one of those World War I planes—something completely open. That would make it easier to drop the bombs. Otherwise, how am I going to get the bombs out of the plane?

January 29

I have bought a fifty-pound bag of peanuts in anticipation of the elephant. I have a history test tomorrow, but I won't be able to study for it because I have to roast the peanuts. With my luck, I'll probably get an elephant that eats only caviar. What do elephants eat? My elephant won't be able to win the race if he or she is dying of starvation. You'd think that for all the money I'm laying out, the guard at the zoo would throw in some food.

January 29—later

I'm worried. Suppose Herdie stuck a regular stamp on the envelope instead of the air-mail special delivery. Why can't he follow orders? Is it too difficult to put the right stamp on the envelope?

No, it's my fault. I should never have trusted the United States Post Office. They're probably searching the envelope right now. All kinds of pornography can go through the mails, but my letter will be seized. Or else, Herdie put the wrong address on it. The key to the lockers is probably on its way to Canada right now.

If that key doesn't arrive soon, I'm really in trouble. I may have a nervous breakdown. The only way I can feel safe is to have that key in my pocket. Lew, on the other hand, doesn't seem nearly as nervous as I am. I don't understand him. I really don't.

It's raining most of the time because of the cloud-seeding business.

January 30—very early

The name of the elephant representing my school is Gladys. The school is very excited about the forthcoming race and every day Montie and I drive to the Sanford Zoo and stand in front of Gladys, talking with her so that she gets used to us. Montie says that when we're with the elephant we should not act suspicious. How do you not act suspicious? Try it. Just try it.

I wonder if Sally is ever going to write me a letter.

Tuesday morning

> It is said Mirabeau took to highway robbery "to ascertain what degree of resolution was necessary in order to place one's self in formal opposition to the most sacred laws of society." He declared that "a soldier who fights in the ranks does not require half so much courage as a foot-pad,"—"that honor and religion have never stood in the way of a well-considered and a firm resolve." This was manly, as the world goes; and yet

> it was idle, if not desperate. A saner man would have found himself often enough "in formal opposition" to what are deemed "the most sacred laws of society," through obedience to yet more sacred laws, and so have tested his resolution without going out of his way. It is not for a man to put himself in such an attitude to society, but to maintain himself in whatever attitude he finds himself through obedience to the laws of his being, which will never be one of opposition to a just government, if he should chance to meet with such.

I'm going to include that passage from Thoreau in my Handbook, though I'm not in agreement about Mirabeau's evaluation of courage. How much courage did my brother, Sam, have when he stepped off that plane, and how would his courage compare to that of an ordinary "foot-pad"? Courage is not measurable. That's what I wrote on my theme for my English teacher, but she only gave me a C for it.

Still, that last part is accurate. The problem for men, of course, is to set up a just government. But there seems to be far too many people. No one government can satisfy them all. One man's just government is another man's fascism. Anarchy. Anarchy.

Tuesday noon

Everything is going as planned. The key has arrived. Nesting safely in locker 347 at the Trailways Bus Terminal in Wilmington, Delaware, is a brown cardboard suitcase with two gray leather straps tied around it. Inside the suitcase rest two small bombs, each weighing approximately twenty pounds. The date of our mission still holds. Lew and I shall strike our blow for the common man on February 26. While the whole country is in the twilight zone between football and baseball, Lew and I will be pitching from the air—inaugurating a new season of our own. I'm glad we have that plane waiting.

Tuesday afternoon

I burnt the roasted peanuts. Do you have any idea what fifty pounds of burnt, smoldering peanut shells smell like? And the peanuts taste worse. Gladys is going to be a very hungry elephant, I think.

January 31

The following schools will race elephants against Gladys: Vassar. Harvard. Yale. The University of Wisconsin. The University of California. The University of North Carolina. The University of New Mexico. That race will be held in the afternoon. In the morning four or five high schools will be racing their elephants. Even high school students can get elephants when they want them. What is this world coming to?

Both *Time* and *Newsweek* magazines will be there to cover the big event, which is going to leave me in an awkward position if the citizens of Sanford decide to get serious about my borrowing their elephant. I think Montie could have made a better deal. Besides, who wants to get up at two-thirty in the morning to pick up an elephant!

February 1

Henry Miller in a letter to Lawrence Durrell: "At sixty-six I am more rebellious than I was at sixteen. Now I *know* the whole structure must topple, must be razed. Now I am positive that youth is right—or the child in its innocence. Nothing less will do, will satisfy."

The whole structure must go. The lid's coming off, baby. A friend of mine returned from Vietnam without any arms and legs. I wonder how he feels now. What does he think about the structure?

And my brother never returned at all. If you give an inch, they'll take the very life away from you, or leave you dying in a hallway somewhere unless you can prove you can pay.

February 2

I would like to get my hands on some hand grenades, but I feel it is a waste of time to try the Army-Navy Store again. The old guy would probably call the cops, and it's too early to get the police involved. Still, I have been watching a John Wayne movie on television, and I love the way he takes a grenade, pulls out the pin with his teeth, and lobs it into a nest of Japanese machine-gunners.

The Yellow Peril once again subdued.

America has always felt threatened by the Yellow Peril, which explains, I suppose, why we call cowards "yellow." Do you suppose that in China, they call cowards *white*? Now, that's the kind of information that should be made available to the general public. That's the kind of thing I am going to include in my Handbook because it keeps us all humble.

February 4

Lew, through some of his friends who are in the Reserve Officers Training Corps at the university—good old ROTC—has brought me a dummy grenade to play with. I've tried to pull out the pin with my teeth, the way John Wayne does, and I have badly chipped two of my front teeth. Now I've got to make an appointment with my dentist as soon as possible because I don't want any distinguishing characteristics upon me when we go up. The key to a good revolutionary is for him to remain anonymous until the precise moment. If he makes his presence felt too soon, it is all over.

 I saw a movie on television once where the criminal was caught because he left teeth marks in an apple. The criminal—I forget who played the part—had bitten into an apple and then carelessly tossed it away. He had neglected the fundamental importance of paying attention to detail, and it turned out that his teeth marks were every bit as good as fingerprints for identification purposes. Therefore, I must get my teeth fixed, and I must remember to wear gloves at all times while boarding and getting off the plane.

Sunday evening

There is a hole in the right-hand pocket of my pants. I must remember not to put the key to the locker in it. A revolutionary must be ambidextrous. But even with all these things on my mind, I feel much better knowing the bombs are safe. If Trailways only knew!

February 5—3 A.M.

Montie and I are parked on a side street next to the Sanford Zoo. We're in the truck that Montie has borrowed from his friend, and for the last hour or so, I have been amazed how well Montie can handle such a monster. I am amazed, and at the same time I am unhappy that I had have had to borrow everything. Borrow the truck. Borrow the elephant. Borrow extra money for a new sack of peanuts. Ownership is nine-tenths of the law, but it is surely ten-tenths of revolutions. The truck says ACE PRODUCE SHIPPING on each side.

"All right. You guys ready?" The guard stands on the running board on Montie's side and peers into the cabin.

"Is Gladys ready?" Montie asks.

"Yeah, she's all ready." The guard is a small pudgy man with a face like a walrus.

Montie opens the door. "Well, then, let's load her on."

"One small hitch though," the guard says.

My heart leaps to my throat. I look around, expecting searchlights to hit us and a thousand cops to jump out of the shadows.

"What's that?" Montie asks calmly. Calmly enough considering the circumstances.

"There's another guy involved and he wants to be paid."

"What do you mean there's another guy involved?" Montie asks, his voice rising. "I told you not to tell anybody."

The guard lights a cigarette. Calmly enough I think, considering the circumstances.

"Look, getting an elephant for a few days isn't like going into the supermarket and getting a can of beans," the guard replies, blowing smoke rings in my direction.

I leap down from the ACE PRODUCE SHIPPING truck. "But you promised." I look at Montie and Montie shrugs his shoulders. We should have brought a gun.

"Well, I kept my promise, didn't I? Gladys is here and in good condition. I couldn't pull it off by myself, and my friend would like a little hush money, if you know what I mean."

"Forget it," Montie says, and gets back inside the truck.

I look at the guard, but I don't say anything. I don't like him very much.

"Come on," Montie says to me.

"What about the money we already gave him?" I ask Montie, who has started the engine.

"Just tell him he's going to be sorry that he double-crossed us."

The guard slaps the side of the truck with his hands. "Look, I'm not double-crossing you. I got the elephant here. I'm just telling you this for your own protection."

"Protection," I say, walking away slowly. It's really disappointing to be so close to winning and yet so far away.

"What about me?" he asks. "I'm laying my job on the line, just so you guys can play some college prank. Why don't you stick to eating goldfish or seeing how many people fit into a phone booth? I didn't ask you to come up here and take our elephant."

He's right, I think to myself. Why did I bother to get mixed up in the whole thing? I have better things to do. I could be back at the school studying my chemistry or my history. Even sleeping would be better.

The guard holds out his arms. "You understand, don't you, kid?"

"Let me talk to my partner," I tell him.

Montie holds the door to the truck partially open. "As far as I'm concerned, there's nothing to talk about. He's got his money, let him deliver the elephant."

"I am delivering her," the guard repeats, removing his cap and wiping his face with his shirt sleeve. "I just would like you to do something for my friend."

"What are we going to do, Montie?" I ask. "I thought you said he'd do it for $300."

"I delivered him his money."

"I didn't say you didn't." Now I'm getting angry at everybody concerned. "Why is he bringing his friend into it?"

Montie stares straight ahead. "Friend! Who does he think he's kidding? He wants to pocket the extra money himself. I say let's forget about the whole thing."

"What about the money we've already given him? The kids at school took up the collection. What am I going to tell them when I come back without the elephant and without the money."

"I'd hate to be in his shoes if the money isn't returned," Montie says loud enough for the guard to hear. "When the guys at the school get through with him, there won't be enough left to feed to the fish."

"Don't threaten me, you punks, or I'll have you all in the clinker," the guard shouts back.

I can't stand the thought of a fight over a simple request, so I tell the guard, "Let me talk with my friend, will you?"

"Hurry it up. I don't have all night."

"Montie, we've got to think of something."

"So think. I'm tired."

The guard is leaning on a link-chain fence. Behind it I can see Gladys standing patiently.

I go over to the guard and ask, "How much does your friend want?"

"Not much. Just a hundred dollars. He's worth it. He gave me a lot of help."

"But I don't have a hundred dollars. We gave you everything we have. You ought to be happy we're taking the elephant. It's not every day you get a deal like this."

"Some deal," he says.

I don't want to give up the elephant, but I can see Montie is ready to drive off.

"Look," I tell the guard. "If Gladys wins, there is a $500 first prize. I don't care about the money. Tell your friend that if we win, you and he can split the money. In other words, you make even more on the deal."

The guard thinks over my offer and crushes his cigarette under his shoe. "OK. If you win, we get the prize money."

"But we keep the trophy," I add. I want something for my effort.

"And you keep the trophy."

We shake hands on it, like the gentlemen we are. "OK. Open up the truck and I'll load her on. You just better take good care of her."

I tell Montie that everything has been settled, but he doesn't look very happy. So I go around to the back of the truck to help with Gladys. She follows the guard slowly and deliberately, waving her great head slowly from side to side. If she can't win the race, I don't know who can.

"You got a flashlight or something?" the guard asks, pausing in front of the ramp. He carries a small prong in his right hand, a piece of wood with a metal hook in it to urge Gladys on.

"What for?"

"Gladys is afraid of the dark. She won't get on the truck unless there's some kind of a light inside to comfort her."

"Are all elephants afraid of the dark?"

"No. Just Gladys. She's a very sensitive elephant."

I get a flashlight out of the glove compartment and set in the back of the van. Gladys gets on without any trouble. I let her take some peanuts out of my hand so we can get re-acquainted.

The guard points back to the fence. "I got a couple of loads of hay back there if you want them."

"Yeah. Thanks." We load the hay on, and I think maybe the guard isn't so bad. I mean, he is risking his job and all.

"Don't let that light go out or you're going to have a problem on your hands."

"Thanks."

We load the hay and I bolt the doors. Maybe I should ride in the van with Gladys, but I really don't want to. I shake hands with the guard, and he wishes us luck in the race.

As I climb into the cabin of the truck, Montie backs out without saying anything, and I think to myself, of all the elephants in the world, of all the elephants I could get, I'd have to get one who's afraid of the dark. I better check the almanac when I get back to the school. If there's an eclipse of the sun on the day of the Great Elephant Race, I'm really going to have my hands full.

Monday afternoon

There ought to be a law against showing John Wayne movies on television. It gives kids false ideas. I don't mean false ideas about the glory. I mean the false idea that you can pull out a hand-grenade pin with your teeth. I know. I tried it, and now I can whistle without even opening my mouth.

I guess I really should go through training of some sort in order to get ready for my mission. I should climb ropes hand over hand. I should run the mile with a pack on my back. I should crawl through acres of mud on my stomach. I must be prepared for any contingency. It may also be useful to know about weapons. If you only knew how sore my mouth is, you would have pity on me.

Still, all is not going badly. I do have an elephant, two bombs, and a plane, quite an achievement considering that I started out this year with a class registration card and two pairs of sheets. Two problems though: the guard at the zoo and Slade. I am dependent on both of them, and this is not a comfortable state of affairs. A leader must be independent. He must not get bogged down in philosophy. He must act out of impulse and insight, though carefully trained impulse and insight. Perhaps I wasn't cut out to be a leader. Certainly my experiences as a monitor in the fourth grade are not a good omen.

All I can see are problems everywhere.

February 6—5 A.M.

When my brother, Sam, was in the ninth grade and I was in the third, the circus came to town and we decided to go. I remember that on the way Sam thought we would save money by buying peanuts from the supermarket instead of from the circus. So we picked up a pound of peanuts. But when we got to the circus we discovered that the peanuts we'd bought were raw. They weren't roasted at all, and raw peanuts taste terrible.

That's what was going through my mind as Montie and I rode back to school with Gladys in the back of the truck. Gladys should only know about all the peanuts I tried to roast for her. They reminded me of that day with my brother.

 Tuesday afternoon

Gladys is such a beautiful elephant and so very well-mannered that I do not wish to keep her cooped up in the truck, though I suppose it is difficult to imagine an elephant being beautiful. A male elephant, though, would be attracted to Gladys. Maybe the race at Chapel Hill will be the beginning of a beautiful romance.

I have placed a stake in the ground right outside my room and have chained Gladys to it. When it begins to get dark, I'll try to rig up some kind of light so that she doesn't get frightened. I would like to practice running the race with her, but I'm not quite sure how to do it. Suppose she starts running and refuses to stop. I'm not going to get in her way, that's for sure. I really would like to know how Harvard and Yale are training their elephants.

Wednesday night

What's happened to the key to the locker? Aspirin. Where's the bottle of aspirin? I think it was John Barrymore who said that in America you buy a lifetime supply of aspirin and use it up in a week. He wasn't kidding either.

February 7

I wonder if I should put Gladys back into the truck and charge people to look at her. That would be one way to earn back some of the expenses. I can't count on any of the prize money, now that most of it has been promised to the guy at the zoo.

The members of the French Club have come by to put their blanket on Gladys—green and white, our school colors. I must say that Gladys will be the best-dressed elephant in the race. Next semester I think I'll take some courses in the business school. That will get me better prepared for the life to come. Give me an elephant and I can move the world. Who said that?

Wednesday morning

I won't be able to get an appointment with the dentist for a month. A whole month! Good thing I'm not coming down with an abscessed jaw or something. I don't understand why a country so rich and powerful can't provide decent medical care for its people. I've already told you that my father was kept in the hospital corridor while my mother fumbled through her purse looking for a Blue Cross card or something to prove that she could pay the bills. Great system, right? How much money will a man pay when he is in pain? He will give away everything he has to get well. Does that sound like a fair basis of negotiation?

At the heart of my revolution will be adequate medical care for all. Perhaps there should be a guaranteed annual income for qualified doctors—say, a hundred thousand a year. Then there should be free medical care for all. Somewhere at the heart of the perfect state is the idea that the citizens of the state are healthy.

First the citizens must be healthy, and next they must be free from fraud. In *Gulliver's Travels,* when Gulliver comes upon the Lilliputians, he soon discovers that

> They look upon Fraud as a greater Crime than Theft, and therefore seldom fail to punish it with Death: For they allege that Care and Vigilance, with a very common understanding, may preserve a Man's Goods from Thieves; but Honesty hath no Fence against superior Cunning: And since it is necessary that there should be a perpetual Intercourse of buying and selling, and dealing upon Credit; where Fraud is permitted or connived at, or hath no Law to punish it, the honest Dealer is always undone, and the Knave gets the advantage.

 When I declare my war, it will say for all to hear that our doctors and our generals, those who should protect us, are practicing fraud upon us.

Wednesday afternoon

Volia. Or *Voila.* Or whatever it is. I don't have time to study for my French exam either. I have to figure out a strategy to use when we meet Slade again. I think I'll open my mouth and make sure he notices my chipped teeth. Then after our mission, when the FBI is looking for a guy with chipped teeth, I'll go to the dentist and have mine repaired. Clever?

Sometimes I get frightened. I have never undertaken anything of such magnitude before. Even the Great Elephant Race seems simple compared to what might lie ahead. Maybe I should include a pep talk with my Handbook. Everybody needs a pep talk once in a while.

Wednesday afternoon—later

"The weapons with which the bourgeoisie felled feudalism to the ground are now turned against the bourgeoisie itself." But who reads Marx nowadays? There are political science majors who don't even read him. Today everything is Che or Mao. But revolutionaries need perspective. One cannot revolt against one's father indefinitely.

Wednesday afternoon—4:30 P.M.

A telegram has arrived, and my heart has stopped in my throat. I don't know why, but telegrams frighten me as much as anything.

This telegram regrets to inform me that because Harvard and Vassar are having transportation problems, the start of the Great Elephant Race has been pushed forward to February 12 from February 8. It really burns me. If I were the one having trouble, they'd go blithely on without me. But since it's Harvard and Vassar, they simply put off the date of the race! What a world. An elephant race should be run according to schedule, with rules designated by the American Olympic Committee. Don't I have any rights at all? I can't even file a protest. I need a lawyer, that's what I need. As soon as a child is born, he should be issued a lawyer and he should be promised a standardized income and a high I.Q.

Now what is that guy at the zoo going to do? If he reports the theft on the seventh as planned, I'm really in trouble. How in the hell am I supposed to hide an elephant? That's what I'd like to know.

Wednesday—5:30 P.M.

I try to relax by thinking about the Pentagon.

The corridors of the Pentagon cover over 17½ miles, and over 27,000 people work there. Actually, that's all I've been hearing for the last few days, because Lew keeps mumbling about how many people work there and how he doesn't want the innocent to suffer. I tell him that in any kind of social upheaval the innocent are the first to go. I then tell him that nobody is innocent. The stupidity, apathy and prejudice of the "innocents" have perpetuated the old guard. It is the innocents who create the order of things in the first place. When the Jews were sent into the gas ovens, who allowed it to happen but the so-called innocents who remained silent, who prayed—yea, fervently prayed that no one would knock upon their own doors, while they closed their eyes to what was happening one door down.

Lew picks up his guitar and begins to ramble off, humming the title song to *The War Between the Worlds,* while in my head I make a memo about faint hearts and chickens. That will make an entire chapter in itself. Still, I retain confidence in Lew. He comes through when the chips are down.

Wednesday evening

I never noticed just how much weight an elephant has to carry on her feet. Gladys' feet swell every time she puts them down, and her feet get smaller when she lifts them off the ground. I could have gone to the zoo a hundred times and not have noticed that. It just goes to show you what it means to have an elephant right in your own home.

Montie hasn't been in a good mood ever since that guard cheated us out of the extra money. I hope he cheers up soon. Gladys could be adversely affected by the prevailing gloom. We must think "Win!" We may not be able to keep the prize money, but there's no law that says we can't bet on our elephant to win. The odds should be pretty good, for I'm certain that Harvard or Vassar is a favorite to win. I just have to keep a careful watch on Gladys to see that she remains in good shape. She likes salt, so I've brought her plenty of salt, and she looks at me affectionately. I think Gladys and I are going to get on pretty good. I have even lit a small fire for her so that she will not be afraid of the dark.

Wednesday night

I have been thinking about Lew's uneasiness. Maybe one effective protest against the Establishment would be to cause rain over the Pentagon every day. We could get some generators on the ground and send up smoke clouds of silver iodide. In that way we could keep the Pentagon under a constant shower. Unfortunately, the protest would be quite expensive, and the rain might be blamed on God anyway. It has to be clear that we are involved in a human protest, a protest of humans on the behalf of humans, and not a heavenly one. God has enough to think about. I am sure that He does not think about the Pentagon.

Near midnight

I am sleeping peacefully in my room when I wake up to the smell of smoke. At first, I think that my roommate has left his cigarette burning in an ashtray, but soon the smoke becomes too strong for that.

Gladys!

I leap out of bed and rush to the window. Sure enough, there is my beautiful elephant trumpeting and shrieking. A couple of bales of hay have caught on fire. It doesn't take too much longer for my roommate to wake up, nor for the rest of the people in the dormitories. I fling open the door and go rushing out. I see Montie a few steps ahead of me. Gladys is tugging at the chain around her left leg and threatens to pull the stake from the ground.

"Montie," I call. "Open the truck. We've got to get Gladys out of here." My roommate and quite a few other members of the dormitory are trying to beat the fire down with blankets, but it is difficult for them to do much good, because Gladys is turning back and forth and is kicking out in panic. Everyone is screaming "Fire!" and that seems to be scaring her. I manage to slip through an opening in the flames and remove the chain from the stake, but the metal is so hot that it burns my hands. Gladys roars and paces back and forth in confusion.

"Hey."

"What the hell is going on?"

"Somebody call the Fire Department?"

"Get some water."

There is confusion all around me as hundreds of my classmates begin to tumble from their beds and rush outside. "Montie," I cry, "Get the truck started." I have to get Gladys out of here before the college administrators arrive. I also have visions of Gladys making a run for it and I have no way of stopping her. I have to get her to safety before she tramples some of my friends.

"Keep calm, girl. It's all right," I tell her, but she can't hear me above her own roaring. Every time someone yells "Fire!" she roars louder and swings her chain.

"Get some hoses and start dousing the buildings before the fire spreads." Alfred Hickley, vice-president of our Freshman Class, has already begun to take charge.

Sensing an opening, Gladys breaks for it, the great weight of her chain clinking uselessly behind her.

"Look out!" A great line of bodies, some in pajamas, some almost nude, parts before the elephant. Nobody is foolish enough to stand in Gladys' way. I try to follow her, but I can't keep pace with her. If Gladys runs this fast in the Great Elephant Race, we'll have no trouble collecting the prize money. Unfortunately, not only will I have to turn the prize money over to the guard at the Sanford Zoo, I may also have to buy a new dormitory for my school. They're brick buildings though. They shouldn't catch fire so easily. If I had only thought for a moment, I wouldn't have placed Gladys and the straw so close to the dormitories.

Gladys has managed to shake herself free from the blanket presented to her by the French Club and has crossed the yard, galloping into the street behind the parking lot. Luckily, Montie is alert, for he pulls the huge ACE PRODUCE SHIPPING truck out and places it in Gladys' path. Gladys thinks twice about running into it and pauses momentarily, allowing me to get into shouting distance.

I don't know what to do. The only thing I can think of is to start singing in the hope that the music will both confuse and soothe her, but the only words that come to mind are the ones to "The Star-Spangled Banner." I start singing our national anthem as loudly as I can, all the while walking slowly and deliberately toward the elephant. Montie has thrown on the headlights so that Gladys won't be afraid of the dark, though it's easy to see because of the flames from the dormitory areas.

Oh say can you see by the dawn's early light
What so proudly we hail . . .

As I approach, singing at the top of my lungs, Gladys stares at me with a dumbfounded expression. Both Montie and I can see that she is beginning to calm down a bit, especially since she's far enough away from the fire.

"Good girl, good girl, everything's going to be all right," I tell her. She trots away from the truck toward the edge of the parking lot, but she doesn't seem to have a destination clearly in mind. I hope she leaves the cars alone. On top of everything else, I don't want to be blamed for wrecking my friends' cars.

"Look, Montie," I say, "I think everything's going to be all right."

"Sure," he says, but he doesn't mean it. He sits in the cab of the truck, his arms and bare chest covered with sweat, and shakes his head from side to side.

"Look," I tell him. "We got to get out of here."

"You're telling me?"

"But I need all the stuff in my room. I've got clothes and peanuts all packed."

"What do you want me to do? I'm not your servant!" Montie snaps.

Montie's tense, so I don't take it personally. "The cops will be here any minute," I say.

"What do you want me to do?" Montie yells. All the time, out of the corner of my eye, I watch Gladys roaming among the automobiles, poking at fenders and radio antennae with her trunk.

"Please, Montie, I've got to watch Gladys. We can't go to North Carolina naked. I've got a lot of stuff in my suitcase."

"I would like to know how that fire started," Montie says viciously.

"How am I supposed to know?"

Montie stares straight ahead, his hands tight on the steering wheel. It's time for action.

"We're going to have to live in the truck for a few days," I say. "Just until things calm down."

"You want me to live with you and an elephant in this truck?"

"Just until I can get a few things straightened out. We'll work it out and hit the road as soon as possible. Then we'll . . ."

"I don't want to hear any more."

"Montie, please, let's hurry. Go get the brown suitcase and whatever stuff you need."

"And what are you going to do, Big Leader?" Montie leaps from the truck and slams the red door behind him.

"I'll get Gladys in the truck. Where's the flashlight?"

"Where do you think it is? It's in the glove compartment where you left it." Montie runs back to the dormitories, where the flames are still flickering, though it doesn't look as serious as it did. I take the flashlight to lure Gladys on board. All I can think of is that the college administration is going to blame me for this fire, and it's not my fault at all. Isn't there any justice in this world?

Thursday morning

Montie couldn't take the smell and so he's temporarily moved in with his friend who owns the ACE PRODUCE truck. Maybe I'm just exhausted, but I'm getting used to it, though I've never been quite so close to an elephant before. It's not so bad really, and Gladys is very easy to get along with. She has calmed down considerably and has eaten a hefty breakfast. If I can just get her to the race, I think things will work out all right.

I'm as anxious as Montie to get on the road, but a new problem has cropped up. I think I've mislaid the key to the locker. It wasn't among any of the clothes rescued from my room. I know I put it in my pants pocket, but I might have put it in the pocket with the hole in it. What is wrong with me? I wasn't always like this. Gladys trumpets at me. I think she wants to go outside for exercise.

I think my life began to go sour when I entered school. My parents sent me to Catholic School for first grade. They thought the discipline would be good for me, but I only remember a couple of things about that whole year. One was that I got a bloody nose for being on the playground with the big boys. A nun dragged me into the infirmary, telling me that I shouldn't have been playing with the big boys in the first place. I learned that when I got my nose bloodied, and so I didn't understand why she had to repeat it. Sam finally came by and walked me home.

I also learned to write with ink, and that almost ruined my life. I'd always get ink on my clothes, but I was only six years old. I don't see what's so terrible about getting ink on your clothes when you're only six years old. That's the trouble with this country. When you're six years old, everybody wants you to be an adult; but when you're ready to be an adult, there isn't any room for you. You can hardly get a decent job, so what's the sense? I'm certainly not going to join the army just to get security.

I look at Gladys standing sleepy-eyed in the truck, swaying her body back and forth as much as she is able to in the cramped quarters, and I know she wants to go outside. We have a lot in common, Gladys and I.

Thursday—1 P.M.

I have found a little lake not too far out of town, and so I have driven Gladys over for a swim. I'm glad that Montie is driving the truck to Chapel Hill, because I don't feel at all comfortable with such a big truck. They're much more difficult to drive than you think, especially when you have an elephant in the back.

I think that water is really Gladys' element. She loves it. She stands on the shore, sucking up water with her trunk and spraying it into her mouth and over her body. I watch her as I paddle out toward the middle of the lake, happy that there is no one around. *"Errraugheow,"* trumpets Gladys from the shore. Soon the lions, the tigers and the leopards will all come down for a drink. If I hadn't lost the key to the locker, it would be a perfect afternoon.

February 9—early in the morning

After much maneuvering, Gladys is fairly comfortable in the truck. Much more comfortable that I am. Actually I would do what Montie did and go off and live with friends, but someone has to keep an eye on our prize. Besides, we're going to hit the road tomorrow, so I can stick it out. Nothing like an elephant to toughen a person.

I would like to get in touch with the guy at the Sanford Zoo, but I'm afraid to stir up trouble. The morning papers don't mention anything about Gladys, so I don't know what's going on with that guy. Maybe the authorities are keeping it out of the papers just to throw me off my guard.

I'll just have to tell Lew about the missing key and he'll have to find it. I can't do everything. That's why I'm a leader. I have followers to do things for me. I don't want to tell Lew, though. Losing the key doesn't reflect well on my ability to lead.

February 10—on the road

Montie and I are driving through Georgia. Gladys is safely in the back of the van, with a flashlight burning to keep her company. Now that we are on the road, Montie is in a slightly better mood, and I'm leafing through my chemistry book. Not studying it, because I don't think they'll ever let me back in class again, just looking at the pictures and thinking what I'm going to tell the administration about the fire. Maybe I should just disappear from the school and not come back. That's the best way I know of dealing with my problems—running away from them. Who wants to look a problem square in the face anyway? I look at the watch I've borrowed from my roommate. Montie and I and Gladys are making good time, considering the confusion we started off in. I want to reach Chapel Hill early so that Gladys will have plenty of time to rest and get used to the track. I'm sure Gladys must be stiff from standing in the truck. I must admit she has a lot of endurance.

I remember seeing a Clark Gable film once where he was a racetrack driver. He got up before daybreak and walked the track to see if there were any holes or bumps. I can still picture him, dressed in a white uniform, kicking here and kicking there. That's what I want to do with Gladys. I don't want her to fall down and break anything. If it's hard to find a decent hospital for humans, think how difficult it would be to get medical attention for an elephant.

"Oh, oh," Montie says.

"What's the matter?" I sit up in the seat and close the chemistry book. A cop is pulling up and waving us over.

"Damn!" Montie is watching the patrol car in his rear-view mirror.

"What are we doing?" I ask.

"Nothing. We've been keeping the speed limit."

Montie, cursing under his breath as only Montie can curse, pulls the truck off the side of the road while the Georgia patrol car stops behind us, its red light spinning. He opens the cab door and jumps down. I hope Gladys knows enough to remain silent.

I sit and wait. It's all I can do. It wouldn't look right for me to join Montie. It might seem as though we were ganging up on the patrolman. I strain to hear what's going on, but I can't make out much of the conversation.

"Ace Produce Shipping, eh?" the patrolman asks. From the mirror I can see that he is a tall thin guy with wavy blond hair.

"What's the matter, officer?" Montie asks. "I thought I was driving under the speed limit."

"Not according to my radar."

"I was only doing sixty."

"What do you have in there?" The patrolman hits the back of the truck with his nightstick.

"Produce."

"I know. I can read. What kind of produce?"

My stomach feels as if Gladys has stepped upon it. I hope Montie comes up with a good answer. If he says the wrong kind of produce we may have to stop for inspection or for weighing.

"Cabbages, lettuce, things like that," Montie says.

"Your boss isn't going to like it if you bring him back a ticket, is he?"

"No, he isn't."

I'm thankful that Montie is being very polite. With a little bit of luck, we will get off with a ticket. If we're very lucky, we'll get a reprimand. It's hard to tell though, because some of these little towns in Georgia are speed traps.

The patrolman takes out his book and Montie hands him his license. I hope Montie remembered to get the registration for the truck.

"Errraugheow."

"What's that?" the patrolman asks, slightly startled.

I think fast and leap down from the cab, all the time imitating Gladys' roar—*"errraugheow,"* I go at the top of my lungs.

"What's wrong with him?" the cop asks, pointing at me.

"That's my friend," Montie says.

"I don't care who he is. What's wrong with him?"

I collapse on the ground.

"Better get him to the hospital," the cop says.

"No. He has these attacks every once in a while, but they pass pretty quickly. Elephantitis."

"Elephantitis?"

"He got it when he was in Africa with the Peace Corps. It'll pass in a minute. Then he'll get up and he won't even remember where he is or what happened to him."

"That a fact?"

"It's unfortunate, but it's a fact."

"You better let me call an ambulance."

Gladys lets out another roar, though from the outside of the truck it sounds quite muffled.

"See, he's coming around," Montie says.

I get up slowly, swinging my head back and forth like an elephant.

The patrolman shakes his head. "Poor kid," he drawls. "That's why I'm not going to let my son join the Peace Corps. There's no telling what disease he may come down with."

"It comes in spells, but it passes quickly," Montie says, staring in my direction, waiting to see what I'm going to do next. My clothes are wringing with sweat.

"Am I far from Nairobi?" I ask, wiping the sweat from my arms and coughing.

"You're all right, Jack."

"You want me to radio for help?" the patrolman asks.

I just get back in the truck as if nothing has happened, silently praying that Gladys will remain still for just a little longer.

"What's he doing with you?" the patrolman asks Montie.

"Oh, I'm doing his family a favor by giving him a ride to the hospital. Ace Produce don't like me to take riders, so if I was speeding, that was the reason. I was in a hurry to get him to the clinic for his checkup."

"Well, you were speeding, but I'll let it go this time."

"Thanks, officer."

"Well, I figure it was worth it for the entertainment." He pulls his shades down and walks back to his car. "You guys better hit the road and get out of my sight before I lose my patience and run you both in. You don't think I'm foolish enough to believe that elephantitis stuff, do you? You just get your produce delivered and watch the speeding. The next time I might not be in such a good mood, and I'll run you both in."

The patrolman climbs in his car, and with his red light still spinning, he drives off down the highway. I never noticed it before, but a police siren reminds me a lot of an elephant roaring.

Montie climbs back into the cab of the truck, his clothes soaked. "Sometimes I don't believe you," he says to me, lighting a cigarette.

"What do you mean, you don't believe me. What did you want me to do? Sit here while that guy ran us in? The Sanford Zoo probably has the FBI looking for us."

"Do you think they know about it up here?"

"How do I know?"

Montie starts the truck up and we're on the road again. This time he's driving more cautiously. I keep my eyes peeled for any signs of policemen behind billboards. "The trouble with you is that you're too pessimistic," I tell Montie.

"That's a laugh. I'm not the one who's pessimistic."

"We're going to win the elephant race and make a bundle. Right?"

"Right."

From the van of the truck, Gladys goes *"Errrraugheow."* I can hear it quite clearly.

Saturday morning—still in the truck

I am still in pursuit of the perfect state. In *Plutarch's Lives,* when the life of the lawgiver Lycurgus is presented, there is this idea:

> Desirous to complete the conquest of luxury and exterminate the love of riches, he introduced a third institution which was wisely and ingeniously contrived. This was the use of public tables where all were to eat in common of the same meat and such kinds of it as were appointed by law. At the same time the citizens were forbidden to eat at home upon expensive couches and tables, to call in the assistance of butchers and cooks or to fatten like voracious animals in private.

Unfortunately, our state has become too large for all of us to eat at a common table, but why should the rich dine on lobsters while the poor are lucky to get hot dogs with rat hairs in them? Who controls the meat prices anyway? I also need to go on a diet, because a fat revolutionary is a contradiction in terms. Besides, I must be in good shape for the exercise ahead. No breakfast tomorrow. No lunch. Maybe some cottage cheese at most. I certainly have no desire to fatten like a voracious animal in private. People in the world are starving while I grow fat.

Saturday—11 A.M.

No trouble getting the revolver. I bought it yesterday from a small store on the outskirts of Atlanta. I have never had a gun before, so it will take some time for me to get the feel of it. This is the real thing, and there is a world of difference between a real gun and the toy ones I used to have as a kid This one can kill a man. I have to be careful with it. I only want to use it as a threat and only as a last resort.

I have called Lew's apartment four times since getting up, but so far I haven't gotten an answer. I suppose it's my fault. When you're a leader, everything gets to be your fault —one way or the other. I know I should not have allowed Lew out of my sight. He probably has a date for the whole weekend, which shows you where his mind is at. My girl friend, Sally, wanted me to see her this weekend but I had to say no. A man must be dedicated. He can't be running around when he's trying to make the world a better place to live in.

I admit that I am not in a very good mood, because I have searched all my belongings that Montie managed to rescue from my room for the key to the locker. But no go. I have looked inside my shoes, my socks, everything. Perhaps my aversion for filing cabinets and briefcases is a bit misguided and slightly infantile, but even if I did possess a filing system, I would file everything under *M* for miscellaneous. I must be better-organized. There is no reason why a world leader can't be as well-organized as anybody else.

Saturday—after lunch

Emerson: "Why are the masses, from the dawn of history down, food for knives and powder? The idea dignifies a few leaders, who have sentiment, opinion, love, self-devotion; and they make war and death sacred—but what for the wretches whom they hire and kill? The cheapness of man is every day's tragedy." And to think, when I was forced to read Emerson in high school, I was bored to tears.

Saturday afternoon

It hits me like a ton of cement. Lew Kemp took the key and hid it. He's out to sabotage the project. That must be it. Otherwise why would the key disappear like that? Perhaps Herdie put him up to it? The thought of Herdie and Lew informing on me fills me with dread. But I have to trust my friends. What are friends for if you can't trust them?

I call Lew again, but there's no answer. In my mind I have narrowed the number of the locker down to three possibilities—473, 347, 734.

Saturday afternoon

There is no 734 at the Trailways station, and both 347 and 473 have keys in them and thus are empty. The cleaning lady at the bus station answered the phone and told me. What reason would she have to lie? So now I know. Lew Kemp has taken the bombs. That's it. I've had it. I'm through. I'm fed up. Enough is enough. Dedication is one thing; fanaticism is another.

Late Saturday afternoon

Montie is worn out from driving the truck, so he wants to go to the movies tonight—to see some lousy detective movie where everyone gets his head blown off, but I'm not going to go. I'm tired of all the violence—and besides, all I can concentrate on is how I've been betrayed. I'm through. I'm fed up. I've had it. I'm going to blow my brains out. That will make everybody sorry.

Saturday evening

I finally reach Lew and I don't believe it! He has taken the bombs to New Jersey to his parents' house and buried them in a flowerbed behind the tennis courts. When I get hold of him I'm going to bury him there, too.

"What in the hell is going on?" I explode at him. "Who gave you the right to take the stuff out of the locker? What did you have to take it out of the locker for?"

"I paid for it. It's mine," Lew says. "I have just as much right to that suitcase as you do."

"I don't care if that suitcase was given to us by God Himself, handed directly down from His throne. Can't you see you're driving me out of my mind? A man can only take so much pressure. I'm flunking out of school, and now this. Don't you know I've got a loaded revolver on me? I can blow off your head in a minute, but even if I did, you'd probably never miss it. Lew, what in the hell is the matter with you? What are you doing this to me for? You know how much time I spent looking for that locker key? I thought I'd lost it. I was climbing the walls for it. But no, you had it all the time and didn't even tell me."

"You thought you lost it?" Lew says. "How could you think you lost it? You gave it to me."

"Don't yell at me," I tell him.

"I'm not yelling at you. You're the one doing all the yelling."

"Was I suppose to admit to you that I might have misplaced the key? I didn't want you upset about it."

"So now you know. You gave it to me."

"Now I know," I tell him, "that the minute I turn my back, you betray me. My best friend, my right-hand man, you have to go off on your own and wreck the whole thing. Is that any way to run a revolution? With everybody running around doing anything he wants? Am I going out of my mind? Am I going insane? Just tell me what you think you're doing? I think you're chickening out on me, that's what I think you're doing. I think you're chickening out on me. What are you going to do? Are you planning to plunge a knife in me the minute I turn my back?"

"Stop talking nonsense, willya? I'm beginning to think you're nuts, calling me like this," Lew says.

"Look, friend, I've got a revolver in my pocket, so just be careful. One more false step from you and I'll blow your brains out. There's no room in our organization for traitors."

"Sure," Lew answers. "Why don't you tell the whole world what's going on? Why don't you keep yelling at the top of your lungs that you're going around with a loaded revolver in your pocket? There are probably eight million people hanging out their windows staring at you right now."

I lower my voice. "Look, Lew, just tell me why you took the stuff out of the locker without telling me?" I can feel that my face is red with anger.

"I didn't want you to worry. I just didn't think that . . ."

"That's it! You just didn't think," I yell at him. I look up and there's a woman waiting to get in the booth. She is carrying a dog, and there are several people staring down at me from windows.

Lew is screaming into the phone. "Will you shut up and let me explain? I thought it over and I didn't think it was too smart to keep the stuff at the bus station. What would happen if somebody decided to break into the locker? Then where would we be, huh? That's what I'd like to know."

"Nobody's going to break into a locker," I tell him.

"Oh no? Those lockers are broken into every Saturday night around here. It's almost a collegiate sport. First you hold up a Seven-Eleven store and then you break into the lockers at the bus station. You know, I'm beginning to think that you're spaced out. It was stupid to put the stuff there in the first place."

"And you're the big brain, I suppose. You win one spelling bee and the world is supposed to fall at your feet."

"I wouldn't make the mistakes you've been making lately. I'm not the one who set fire to the dormitories."

"That wasn't my fault either. Somebody must have tossed a cigarette into the hay."

"Look, forget about it," Lew says.

"I'm taking care of this plan," I shout. "You understand? I'm taking care of it. You're Trotsky to my Lenin; you're Humphrey to my Johnson. You follow me into the Valley of Death with not so much as a whisper. You had no right to do what you did. I don't care what you say. Now everything's fouled up."

"Shut up," Lew says, "or I won't pay for the plane."

"Don't threaten me with your capitalist atrocities. Your father's money is tainted with the blood of innocent workers. Your family has squeezed the life out of the workers to get money into the cash registers."

"The trouble with you, Charlie," Lew says angrily, "is that you're fighting the wrong revolution. The Revolution you're fighting has been fought a long time ago. Get with it, Charlie. You're just not with it."

"My name's not Charlie."

"To me it is. You're trying to drag nineteenth-century values into the middle-twentieth century and it just won't work."

"Oh yeah?"

"Yeah."

"Oh yeah?"

"Yeah."

"We'll see about that." I hang up, leaving Lew wrapped in his anger. The woman with the dog in her arms is staring at me.

Montie says his head is cracking open and he needs diversion very badly. "OK," I say, "let's go to the movie." It has to be a drive-in movie, though. I'm not leaving Gladys alone. The Monroe Doctrine of Revolutions: Beware of entangling alliances. I know I've said it before, but it bears repeating.

Saturday evening at the movies

The detective is climbing the stairs, leaping over the corpse of the landlady, who has been strangled by the Midnight Murderer. His gun blazes. The Midnight Murderer falls over the banister, his shirt covered with blood. The audience howls. They're glad to see it happen because he deserved his fate—if ever a man deserves his fate.

Mentally I compose a letter to a friend of mine who's being sent to jail for defying the government: "Dear Jim. You do not know how much anguish your own anguish is causing me, and yet at the same time, for all your ordeal, I rejoice a bit. I rejoice that there is at least one man with a conscience in our country, at least one man who knows how to say no. When I declare war it will be in your name and in the name of my brother, Sam, whom you just barely knew, as I barely knew. But you I know, and now I know you better."

Somebody has hit the detective on the head with the back of a shovel. It looks almost all over for him, but he's the star. The producers can't afford to let anything happen to a star.

Sunday

The sun has come out and nobody can wish for a better day. I try to think more about the perfect state, but it's too beautiful a day and my thoughts go around in circles. I should write a letter to my friend Jim, but I can't remember all the wonderful things I thought of while I was watching the movie. Watching a movie it is easy to think of beautiful letters; when you're sitting there, everything you think is beautiful and wonderful. And then the movie ends, and everything you've thought of just disappears.

I call Lew. He's suffering from a mild hangover, but he apologizes for taking the suitcase out of the locker, and we fume and haw for about half an hour. I apologize to him for the things I said about his father, and I finally take him back into the fold. Why shouldn't I take him back? I need him to pay for the rental of the plane—and besides, the bombs are buried in his flowerbed. Even a revolutionary has got to be practical some time. The very fact that he has taken the trouble to answer my phone call indicates that his involvement with our symbolic protest is sincere and committed. I know I couldn't go through the thing alone. I need to have someone with me who knows a little something about planes.

Lew and I talk about the plan. The real hang-up at the moment is the parachutes. We must both know how to jump from the plane just in case Slade refuses to land us after we've dropped the bombs. That's always a possibility. I wish Lew knew more about flying.

My advice is that we practice rolling and tumbling. I agree to meet him after the elephant race and then hang up. I'd call Sally, but I don't have any more change.

Sunday

Thomas Hobbes: "THE RIGHT OF NATURE, which Writers commonly call *Jus Naturale,* is the liberty each man hath, to use his own power, as he will himself, for the preservation of his own Nature; that is to say, of his own Life; and consequently, of doing anything, which in his own judgement and reason, he shall conceive to be the aptest means thereunto."

Sunday noon

Montie, in spite of his bad mood, drives carefully and we don't get pulled over by any more patrolmen. Considering all the stops we've made, we reach Chapel Hill, North Carolina, in fairly good time, and I am quite optimistic about the outcome of the race. Optimistic, I said, and not pessimistic, the way my fifth-grade teacher would label me. I am beyond labels now.

We drive around the town a bit and over to the college, and after several different sets of directions from a number of students, we find the fairgrounds where the Great Elephant Race is to be held. When Montie pulls the Ace Produce truck onto the lot, there are already a number of people present to greet us and help us get registered. It costs me an additional $15 registration fee to make Gladys eligible for the bonus race, and one of the girls informs me that tomorrow morning at ten o'clock a veterinarian will show up to give the elephants a thorough examination. I suppose I'll have to tip him, too, although the examination is a good idea. Nobody can afford to have his elephant drop dead on him. It's hard enough to figure out what to do with a live elephant. What can you possibly do with a dead one?

Montie and I make the rounds of the fairgrounds, peering into trailers and talking with our rivals from the other schools and colleges. Some of the elephants I've seen look much larger than Gladys does, but that's OK with me. Extra weight can certainly be no advantage. The one from Berkeley seems to be enormously large. The crew that transported him must be intelligent to get their elephant from California to North Carolina. I wouldn't know how to do it at all. Compared to the Berkeley elephant, and to some of the others, Gladys is lithe. *Lithe.* Yes, that definitely is the word for Gladys.

Sunday

Hitting Slade over the head with the revolver is the part of the plan that I like least, although I know it must be done. What else can I do? Slade isn't going to let us drop the bombs out of his plane without trying to stop us—old chiptooth and the boy with the light-sensitive eyes. If he remains unconscious for a while, it will give Lew and me a chance to get away. There's really no way out of hitting Slade because a despicable world demands despicable acts. I comfort myself by thinking of our own revolution against the British. Who in his right mind would say that he himself is a murderer at heart?

Sunday afternoon

We're not on the lot for more than two hours, and Montie has struck up a friendship with a girl from Vassar. I must admit that they have hit it off well. Montie's like Lew in that respect. They both do well with girls. If there's a secret to it, I wish they'd let me in on it. So, while I'm in the van of the Ace Produce truck, clearing it out, Montie and his new girl friend are off somewhere. Quite a few of the elephant teams are throwing parties, and I have to admit that everyone on the lot seems friendly, but I don't want to abandon Gladys. She might get frightened.

I'll tell you one thing, though. Gladys' personal habits leave a lot to be desired. She has certainly made a mess of the van. I hold my nose and go in with a shovel. In any other competitive circle, my actions would come under the heading of the will to win.

"Gladys," I say, "why couldn't you wait? You knew I was going to take you for a walk." Gladys sways back and forth, staring at me with those big sorrowful eyes of hers until my heart nearly breaks.

February 11—late at night

The rules for the Great Elephant Race:

1) February 12, at 9 A.M., the contestants will present their elephants to Dr. Hardwell for examination. Any elephant that has been administered any form of drug will be immediately disqualified. The winning elephant will be examined after the race.
2) The Great Elephant Race will begin promptly at three o'clock for the college division and at four o'clock for the high school division. There will be a $500 first prize in each division. The two winning elephants will be placed in a match contest at five o'clock. There will be a $250 bonus prize for the match contest. Winner take all.
3) Elephants must not be allowed to run loose on the fairgrounds.
4) Elephants must be accompanied by their trainers or by a team member at all times.
5) During the race, the trainer or team member may carry no stick, club, prodder, or whip of any kind.

Anyone carrying such instruments in his or her hands during the race will be automatically disqualified.

6) Elephants may wear blankets or other decorations. Elephants may be painted or dyed, but may not wear bells or any sound-making device which could distract the other contestants.
7) Stuffed animals or pictures of any sort (especially mice) may not be placed upon any elephant.
8) Elephants shall not wear skates, skate boards, nor shall they be motorized in any way.
9) By order of the Police Department of Chapel Hill, there will be no gambling on the fairgrounds.
10) No profanity may be written on the elephants.
11) In all matters affecting the Great Elephant Race, the decision of the judges will be considered final.

NOTICE TO PRESS:

Information and publicity releases, including photographs, are available from Miss Ima Schetmer in Tent Area One.

While I'm studying the rules, somebody knocks on the van of the truck.

"Who is it?" If it's the Police Department, I'm sunk.

"Paul Arsk from the *Daily Tarheel*—the school newspaper. I'd like to get a picture of you with your elephant."

"How about tomorrow?" I ask, thinking that I don't want my picture taken with Gladys until the race is over. "I'm dead-tired right now. Can you come back tomorrow?"

"Can't. Got classes."

"I'm sorry. Not now. Miss Schetmer in Tent Area One has a picture of Gladys. I sent it in with the application."

"Not the same. You're not with her."

"Sorry. Later."

"OK."

After the photographer leaves, I have pangs of regret. If Gladys wins, I won't even have a picture of us together.

February 12—day of the Great Elephant Race

Gladys and I are up early, six o'clock in the morning, in fact. And the two of us are walking the track, while I patiently explain how she is to pace herself, how she is suppose to come to the outside of the pack and then sprint ahead at the last moment. Elephants are supposed to have good memories, but I repeat the instructions to her four or five times so that she won't forget. She seems to understand what I'm telling her, but how can I be certain? Even I don't understand what I'm talking about half the time. I promise her a lot of salt if she wins. Like humans, elephants understand rewards.

February 12—the names of the elephants

I'm studying the opposition, but it's not exactly like a horserace because there is no information on how they have run before. The opposition is:

Rabbi Ben Ezra — Harvard University
Ms. Margaret Fuller — Vassar
The Good Humor Ice Cream Man — Berkeley
Male Chauvinistic Elephant — Bryn Mawr
The Five Chinese and the Elephant — The University of Wisconsin
Starry Night — Yale University
Dumbo — University of North Carolina (Chapel Hill)
Smoking Is Not as Bad for Your Health as Getting Stomped by an Elephant — Duke University
Frankincense and Myrrh — Wake Forest

As I read over the names, I realize that "Gladys" might be too simple. Perhaps she could use a name that is slightly more exotic. The team from Yale calls its elephant Starry Night because a piece of its left ear is missing. Their elephant is borrowed from Barnum and Bailey, because one of the students is related to the men who own it. A couple of people have asked me where I got my elephant from, but I remain silent.

Gladys. The trouble is that if I change her name at this late date she might get confused. As the Bible so clearly states, there is a time to take chances and a time not to take chances.

February 12—breakfast

Montie finally wakes up and crawls out of his friend's tent to tell me about the contacts he has made. Not just female contacts, but about people interested in wagering on the outcome of the race. Most of the teams don't feel averse about betting a few dollars on the side, and there is even a local bookie in town who's taking some of the action. The odds are a little erratic to say the least, but nobody seems to mind much, since it's all good clean fun.

As Montie points out, if the kids who rounded up the elephants weren't gamblers, they wouldn't be here in the first place. I confess that I have to agree with him. And so the betting, in spite of Rule 9, has started. Montie and I are betting slightly more than we have, but so what? We only live once.

February 12—10 A.M.

Gladys and I have run the eighth of a mile in pretty good time. But I don't want Gladys to give her best yet, especially not under the eyes of the opposition. During the practice sessions, I want her to hold back a little. But I'm not worried. Nobody here has ever raced against a lithe elephant before.

February 12—11 A.M.

The report is that the organizers of the race are disappointed that there aren't more elephants entered in the events. But what could they expect? They should be pleased at the turnout they have. Do they think elephants grow on trees?

February 12—noon

After a long wait in line, Gladys has passed her physical with flying colors, which means that we are more than halfway home. Montie claims that we stand the chance of making a pot of money.

February 12—1 P.M.

Quite a few elephant jokes are going around, so many that I am getting sick of them.

> How many elephants can you fit into a Volkswagen?
> The answer is four. Two in the front seat and two in the back.

There are others, but I'm sure you've heard them all already.

February 12—2 P.M.

Two or three kids from school have sent Montie and me telegrams wishing us luck. I think that's pretty good of them, for I really hadn't expected any at all. There's even one all the way from South Dakota, from a good friend of Montie's. That's really nice, I think. Nothing from Sally, though. There are many things about me Sally doesn't understand.

I lead Gladys up to the starting line and am amazed by how many people there are in the stands. There must be a couple of thousand, and don't you know that Gladys looks pretty in the blanket made for her by the French Club. Our post position is Number 5, between Male Chauvinistic Elephant and The Five Chinese and the Elephant, but before we reach the post position—actually just some white lines marked in lime on the grass—the Elephant from the University of Wisconsin, a female elephant like Gladys, sneaks up and tries to bite Gladys' tail off.

"Hey, what's going on here?"

"Get your elephant out of the way."

"Move the elephant."

"Errraugheow," Gladys roars and turns to bite the tail off the Wisconsin elephant. The dust is flying and a few of the other elephants have begun to retreat. I look helplessly toward Montie, but neither of us knows what to do. Who wants to go in there and break up two fighting elephants?

"Gladys, stop that."

"Back, girl."

"Somebody bring me a stick."

A girl from Berkeley throws a bucket of water over the elephants, soaking not only Gladys but me. One of the policemen takes out his gun and is going to fire into the air, but somebody catches him in time. The shot might scare the other elephants as well.

"Gladys," I shout as loudly as I can, but it takes a lot of yelling because the two elephants are roaring and trumpeting. There's so much dust in the air, I get the feeling I'm in the middle of a sandstorm. Why does this have to happen to me? All I wanted to do was to lead my elephant to the starting line, run the race, collect the money, and go meet Lew without any fuss and bother.

The University of Wisconsin team finally throws a blanket over the head of their elephant, and after much back-and-forth maneuvering and shouting, The Five Chinese and the Elephant is led away. An announcement is made that there will be a slight delay in the race until some new post positions can be assigned.

I check Gladys to make sure she is still all right. I'm proud of her because she managed to hold her own. I'm proud of her, but I don't tell her so. "Gladys, aren't you ashamed of yourself?" I ask, but Gladys doesn't look ashamed at all. Montie discovers a few minor bruises, but at least Gladys' tail is still intact and she will still be able to run the race. We breathe a sigh of relief, thankful that the fight was only a skirmish, thankful that we didn't have to go between the elephants and try to separate them.

Sunday afternoon—3:15 P.M.

A few facts about the Pentagon to be included in the Handbook I am writing:

Built in 1941–42, the Pentagon houses under one roof the United States War Department offices. The building covers approximately thirty-four acres of land and was built at an initial cost of $83,000,000. It is often referred to as the world's largest office building. I am sure that it is often referred to by other names as well.

The structure, built of steel and reinforced concrete, consists of five concentric pentagons and eighteen spokelike main corridors which connect the five floors. Approximately 30,000 people are employed in this building, and thus the Pentagon must contain a complex of support services. In addition to its war-rooms, conference tables, and body-count statistics, the Pentagon contains a shopping center larger than two football fields, a heliport, a bank, etc. Approximately 45,000 telephones can also be found within its walls, so it seems reasonable to assume that the money used to pay the monthly telephone bill could feed the entire population of Des Moines, Iowa, for at least a week. I'm not at all sure about that last statistic because I made it up, but it is a fact that the Pentagon has a parking lot for over 8,000 automobiles.

The perimeter wall of the Pentagon is faced with Indiana Limestone.

Such is the nature of our target.

February 12—3:30 P.M.

The race is on. Come on, Gladys. Come on. Be lithe. Be swift. May your great, though attractive, elephant legs be like the flight of the hummingbird. Rabbi Ben Ezra takes the lead, followed by The Good Humor Ice Cream Man. Ms. Margaret Fuller from Vassar is in third position, and Gladys is holding her own at fourth, followed closely by Male Chauvinistic Elephant and Starry Night. I'm afraid that the University of Wisconsin Elephant is going to catch up with Gladys and then, if those two temperamental females begin fighting again, where will we be? I'll be out a lot of money, with creditors breathing down the back of my neck. That's where I'll be.

The weather is good, with a cool breeze blowing from the southeast. The track is fast. Few people realize how fast an elephant can run if it really has to.

About a quarter of the race is already over and Rabbi Ben Ezra falls back, overtaken by The Good Humor Ice Cream Man. I'm cheering my lungs out, along with Montie and thousands of other fans. I keep yelling to Gladys, "Fire! Fire!" thinking those words will have a stimulating effect upon her, no matter if they have a confusing effect on the people around me. "Fire!" As soon as Gladys of the Sorrowful Eyes hears that key word, she remembers (I think. Who dares to predict what goes on in an elephant's mind?) her terrifying experiences at the dormitories and takes off, faster than I have ever seen her run.

"Errraugheow," goes my elephant, actually the Sanford Zoo's elephant, in recognition. I hope it's recognition rather than panic.

I look back toward the starting line, for I had run ahead with Gladys at the start, and there are the Duke University students pleading with Smoking Is Not as Bad for Your Health as Getting Stomped by an Elephant. They can't get their elephant off the ground. He refuses to run. There but for the grace of God go Montie and I.

Dumbo and Yale's Starry Night are pulling toward the outside. Outside. That's where I want Gladys to go, otherwise she's going to be jammed, crowded out by Ms. Margaret Fuller and Male Chauvinistic Elephant, and when an elephant gets crowded out, she really gets crowded out. The guy standing next to me gets so excited that he spills his Coke on me, but I don't care.

Montie, who is posted at the halfway mark, now takes up the strategy yell of "Fire! Fire!" Gladys responds to Montie's voice and picks up steam, lifting her fat little legs. A guy in front of me, in a Wake Forest sweat shirt and dungarees, is jumping up and down, rooting for Frankincense and Myrrh. I don't like people who aren't rooting for the same things I am. "Why don't you pray for him," I tell him.

I can see it's difficult to keep some of the elephants on the track. At least greyhounds have a little mechanical rabbit to follow and horses have jockeys to guide them. Starry Night, with its damaged ear flapping like a small gray flag, tries to leave the field, but members of the Yale team wave their arms and hands in the air, and get their respective entry onto the track. If Gladys tries to leave, I don't think I'll be able to stop her.

Rabbi Ben Ezra begins to slow down, so the Harvard team begins shouting lines of poetry to encourage it:

The curfew tolls the knell of parting day,
  The lowing herd wind slowly o'er the lea,
The plowman homeward plods his weary way
  And leaves the world to darkness and to me.

"Hey," I call to them, "stop it. You're confusing my elephant." If they don't stop reciting their poems, I'll have to lodge a complaint with the organizers of the event. I'll have a foul called against them. If they want to yell words of encouragement, that's all right with me. But an entire poem? No go. Not on your life.

Farther up the course, in a swirl of dust, Montie is shouting "Fire! Fire!" and some of the spectators are beginning to get confused.

"Get the Fire Department," somebody yells.

"Where's the fire?"

"I don't see a fire."

If Gladys doesn't win soon, we're going to cause a panic. That will make a bizarre headline: ELEPHANTS TRAMPLED BY STAMPEDING HUMANS.

I strain my neck to see what's going on, when I feel somebody tapping me on the elbow.

I jump down to get a better view. "Leave me alone," I say to whoever is tapping me.

"Are you Theodore Jonathan Wainwright?"

"Never heard of him."

"All right, come along with us." Somebody grabs me by the arm, spinning me around. I almost fall over into the crowd, but somebody holds me. There are two men in suits, one of them flipping open an alligator wallet and flashing a badge in my face, its cold metal against my nose. "Police," he says.

"No kidding."

"Come along quietly."

The crowd is still cheering for the elephants, as if nothing is happening, and nothing is happening—to them.

"At least let me see the end of the race in there," I plead. "That's my elephant up there."

The guys walk me toward the edge of the fairground. They won't have any of my argument. "That elephant doesn't belong to you."

"The lithe one?" I hope Montie can see what's going on so he can make his escape before it's too late. If they search the truck and find the gun, it's really all over.

I glance back over my shoulder, but I can't see anything of the race.

Monday evening—8 P.M.

There is only one government that is dominating the world today and that is the government of bureaucracy and red tape. Fill out this form. Take this number. Please be seated. The Pentagon, with its elaborate budgets, represents bureaucracy and red tape as well as anything on this globe. The police are a good model, too.

Monday—later

"I can't understand why everybody's making such a big deal about a practical joke, a college prank. So I borrow an elephant for a few days to run in a race. Is that a crime against humanity? Ask the elephant. She's probably never been so happy in her life. At least she's not kept behind bars all day."

The man in the brown suit just stares at me.

When I talk to my parents on the phone, all I get is more grief. Not only are they all upset about the theft of the elephant from the zoo, but they've also received a special-delivery letter from the Dean of Students of my school, a letter informing them that I have been expelled for setting fire to a dormitory.

Now I know what it's like to be in the movies, yelling,

“I didn’t do it, copper. I didn’t do it. I’m telling you that I’m going to get out and track down whoever did.”

And then the bars clank shut behind him.

February 13

My parents call again and keep asking me why I can’t be more like my brother, Sam, and how Sam never gave them any trouble like this. And I ask, what trouble? It’s only a little prank. Burning down the dormitory is no prank, they say. I didn’t burn down the dormitory, I tell them. Somebody must have thrown a cigarette into the straw. Stop lying, they say. Who am I covering up for? I’m not covering up, I tell them. And stop reminding me of Sam. My parents say it might be good for me to stay in jail for a few days. I say, do you like rats? Do you like sleeping in a mattress that someone has urinated in? I’ll wire you some money, my father says.

The conversation ends.

February 13—later

Montie hasn’t shown up yet, so I guess that means he’s gotten away. I hope he has enough sense not to come see me, since he can’t do anything to help me. I hope he goes back to the Sanford Zoo and smashes in the face of that guard. That guard has really betrayed us. And after giving him all that money.

February 14—early morning

Lew came through with bail. I called my father and said not to bother about the money, which has upset him as much as my getting thrown into jail in the first place.

Anyway I'm out and I'm not hanging around. I'm off to Lew's house. I'll show them. I'll show everybody. Such a big deal over nothing. Who gives anybody the right to own an elephant anyway?

February 16

I spend an hour talking with Herdie about the possibility of getting a plastic bomb, an explosive that can be more easily hidden than an incendiary bomb. A plastic bomb filled with RDK, but Herdie tells me that only a powerful detonator can set it off. I have to be satisfied with what I have, with what he's made for me. The rest of the evening is spent with Lew Kemp. We've settled our differences of opinion, and now we're back on the track again, our revolutionary goal in sight.

Lew and I, practicing for the parachute jump, jump off a small shed behind the tennis courts. We jump, we land, we roll, we jump, we land, we roll. We jump. We land. We roll. We jump. By eleven o'clock, we're both tired, both covered with dirt and bruises. I may be so sore that I won't be able to walk tomorrow. But if we have to parachute, we might as well be prepared for it. There is the always the possibility that Lew might be able to land the plane for us if Slade won't. But who can count on that? I don't think a reasonable man would risk it.

February 17

Our school newspaper, actually my ex-school newspaper, had arrived in the mail and there on the back page is a report of the elephant race. Gladys has won, bless her heart, beating out Rabbi Ben Ezra and The Good Humor Ice Cream Man. Unfortunately, the police had captured her, so that she wasn't allowed to run in the playoff race against Rumplestiltskin from Morristown High. Cheated out of an easy $250.

I have no idea how Montie got away. The paper doesn't mention that. Maybe the girl from Vassar rescued him. I hope so, though I still don't understand the treatment I got. Am I living in a society that has lost its sense of humor along with its values? I wonder what happened to my clothes and my gun.

February 19

Lew has managed to get me another gun. His father had one hidden away in his bedroom, stuffed in a dresser drawer. It's a small revolver, but it will have to do. Lew has taken it without telling anyone. His father won't miss it. Next on the agenda is to get me another suit and more disguises. New rule: When outfitting a revolution, buy two of everything.

February 21

To my fellow students, I'm a hero. To the administration, I'm an outcast. Let it be remembered, though, that we beat Harvard, Yale and Vassar in the Great Elephant Race of the century. That's no mean feat. No one else has the gumption to go out and get an elephant. A lithe one at that. There must be somebody who can make use of my initiative.

My only alternative now is to try to get into a new school. Maybe the University of Delaware will take me. I couldn't bear going home and listening to my parents tell me how good Sam was. There's a lot about Sam they don't know, that I won't tell, that I will never tell anybody.

Sunday night—2 A.M.

"There are two elements of importance and influence among mankind," John Stuart Mill writes: "the one is property; the other, powers and acquirements of the mind. Both of these, in an early stage of civilization, are confined to a few persons. In the beginnings of society, the power of the masses does not exist; because property and intelligence have no existence beyond a very small portion of the community, and even if they had, those who possessed the smaller portion would be, from their incapacity of co-operation, unable to cope with those who possessed the larger." Right on. Right on. I read it two or three times, but it still does not put me to sleep.

I keep thinking that I need 13.2 pounds of plutonium and about 20 kilograms of enriched uranium. Not only is the anticipation of tomorrow keeping me awake, but there is also a slight pain in my left ankle. I might have sprained it leaping from the shed.

Suppose the bombs don't go off? Suppose Slade doesn't show up?

I repeat to myself the facts that the outer perimeter of the Pentagon is faced with Indiana Limestone, and that the basic materials needed to build an atomic bomb in your own basement are 13.2 pounds of plutonium and 20 kilograms of enriched uranium. Who has the right to buy and sell the minerals in the earth and to use them for such destructive purposes?

Outside it is beginning to rain.

Monday—D-DAY

It is raining. I knew it would rain today, but I refused to admit it to myself. I am always amazed how well I persist in the direction of self-delusion. It's not a downpour, just a drizzle, but that's bad enough in its own way. In addition there's a good wind blowing. I'm not even sure that experienced parachutists would jump on a day like this. I know you have to allow for wind. But how much? Thank God the Pentagon is such a large structure, or our bombs might end up in Delaware.

Both Lew and I look like two businessmen going on our daily shuttle flight to Chicago, except for the fact that Slade's plane doesn't look exactly like a DC-7. Winnie Mae actually looks pathetic on the runway, waiting for us to board her. The red clay has turned to mud, and the mud is getting inside my shoes and onto the cuffs of my new pants.

"So you guys showed up anyway," Slade says. "I didn't know if you'd like to go up on a day like this. Here." He shoves a dog-eared pamphlet into Lew's hands.

"What's this?" Lew asks. He turns the pamphlet over and looks at a picture of the White House. It's a tourist guide to Washington, D.C.

Slade takes out a cigarette and lights it, all the while looking at the sky, searching for a break in the weather. "I found that copy lying around the house the other night. My old lady bought it for me before I joined the Army, so I thought you might like it. I mean, you being new to the United States and all."

Lew flips through the pages. It's an old pamphlet all right. Some of the pages have turned brown at the edges. There's no picture of the Pentagon in it, of course. As the three of us walk across the field to where Winne Mae is, Lew looks at me, and I look at the ground. I guess we're both touched by Slade's thoughtfulness.

"You want it back?" Lew asks.

"No. Me and the old lady know our way around by now, and the kids have gone."

"How many?" I ask.

"Five."

"That's a fairly large family."

"You telling me? Kept me hopping to feed them, but they turned out all right, though. Got one in the Army somewhere," he says, his voice trailing off. He shrugs his shoulders. "I'm not much of a one for writing letters, but they all turned out all right."

I find it difficult to imagine what Slade's old lady is like, or even what kind of home he lives in. To look at him you would think he didn't have a home, only a plane.

In my Handbook, however, I must make a note of general principles: Only two things can defeat a revolutionary —mediocre planning and sentimentality. Planning and strategy can be taught, but sentiment must be strangled in the womb. It is the throats of our own parents we must cut. I will ignore Slade and his travel book.

"Do you think it's safe to go up on a day like this?" I ask. Slade opens the door to Winnie Mae and brushes some potato chips off the front seat.

"This little drizzle won't bother nothing." He points at the luggage. "Whatja bring a suitcase along for?"

I'm lost for an answer. I look at Lew. Lew says that he's got a train to catch as soon as we land and that he won't have time to go back to the apartment.

"Well, no sense carrying it up if we're coming back here anyway. Let me put it inside the hangar for you. It'll be safe there. Nobody'll bother it."

Slade reaches a helpful hand for the suitcase containing the bombs, but Lew ignores it. He lifts the suitcase and quickly gets into the back seat of the plane. "No," Lew says. "I'll just sit with it in the back seat. It's not too heavy. And everything I own is in there, you know."

Slade nods. He knows.

I look Lew straight in the face. "No, let me sit in the back seat with it," I say. "I can see Washington any time. You ought to be comfortable so you can concentrate on the sights."

"No, that's all right. I'll sit with it."

"No," I tell him, "I'll sit with it." I try to grab the suitcase out of Lew's hands, but he won't let go of it. We have a small tug of war between us. I realize that I must not allow this dispute to get out of hand or else Slade will begin to suspect something. At the moment he's staring at us as if we were out of our minds. I'm trying to be gentle, because I don't know how much juggling and shaking will set off the explosives. I get a good grip on the suitcase and give it a yank. I didn't realize that Lew had decided to let go of it, so I'm taken with surprise. More than surprise. I lose my balance and topple backward out of the plane and into the mud. But I have the suitcase. A small step backward for me, but a giant step forward for mankind.

Slade comes running over to help me, his big arms swallowing me up as he stands me on my feet again. "You've ruined your suit," he says. "Maybe I can find something to brush it off."

"That's all right," I tell him. "I'll change when we get back."

Slade scratches his head. "Look, why don't you go inside the men's room and change. Your friend must have something in the suitcase for you to wear."

"There isn't," I say. "He isn't even my size."

Slade is so concerned I can't look at him anymore. He's still trying to brush the mud off my suit, but realizing that I am beyond advice, he says, "Well, it's up to you."

Lew takes out his checkbook and writes Slade a check. It's a good maneuver, for it takes Slade's attention away from me and the suitcase.

"Move up front," I tell Lew. There comes a time when a leader must lead and a follower must follow. If the followers begin to lead, everything will fall into confusion. Lew mutters something under his breath and I climb into the back seat with the suitcase. I realize that I am in slight pain because, when I fell, I fell on the revolver in my coat pocket and bruised my hip. Next time I'll strap the revolver to the side of my leg and then there will be less chance of injury. I place my hand to my mouth to adjust my mustache. It's coming loose.

"You know, I've been thinking," Slade tells us. "A friend of mine—George Vorhees—he's got a Cessna Twin Engine Executive. I could borrow that if you prefer."

Now that I'm settled I'm not moving for anyone. "No," I say. "We're anxious to get started."

"This is fine," Lew says.

"I just wanted you to know, that's all. I myself prefer Winnie Mae because she's a lot more fun, and I thought you kids would get a kick out of it."

"Yeah," I say. *Kids.* We'll show him. I settle back and put my hand in my coat pocket to make sure that the gun is still there. If Slade tries to louse us up, I'll have to get rough with him. I don't want to get rough with him, but he better watch out.

Slade takes his position in the cockpit and adjusts his headgear, a ratty brown helmet right out of the old World War I movies. Then he presses the starter.

"What about the parachutes?" I ask him.

"Huh? What did you say?" The roar of the propellers is almost deafening.

"Where are the parachutes?" I shout.

"I don't know. They're in the back somewhere."

He seems very cavalier about taking my life into his hands. After all, I've never been up in a private plane before. I wonder if I'm dressed warmly enough, for I hadn't anticipated falling into the mud.

"I'm not going up without a parachute on," I tell him.

"Are you kidding?" Slade asks with a pained expression on his face.

"No, I'm not."

"Everybody I take up goes up without a parachute. They're there if we need them." The throttle is fully opened, and Slade is taxiing forward, maneuvering a bit with the rudder.

"I'm afraid of heights as it is. We can't go up without a parachute," I tell him.

"All right, all right. Reach behind you and get them."

I reach behind me and get the parachutes and pass one up to Lew. Lew doesn't look very happy, and I'm beginning to sweat because of the humidity. The sweat makes it that much more difficult for me to keep my mustache in place.

We taxi around for a while. "These old girls have got to warm up before they're ready," Slade explains.

"Mr. Klusewzki . . ."

"Call me Slade."

"Slade, is there anything we should know?" I ask him. There's a lot *he* should know, but a revolution is a one-way street. Once you've started there's no turning back.

"About what?"

"About emergencies," I say. "In case something should go wrong."

"Nothing's going to go wrong."

"What if it does?" I say, but even Slade's patience has its bounds.

"Look, I've gotten no complaints yet. Just sit back and enjoy yourself. If you're uncomfortable, it's because you've got mud all over yourself."

"The rain is letting up," Lew says, trying to change the subject. I've got to hand it to Lew. He's playing heads-up ball.

"What if the plane catches fire?" I ask. My mustache is loosening.

"Whatja say? I can't hear what you say if you keep your hand in front of your mouth all the time."

I rub the mustache back in place. Next time I'll just grow one. My question about fire comes to mind again because of the blue flames spitting from the engines, but I decide against pursuing it. I can't afford to get Slade annoyed. Lew isn't saying much, just looking at his guidebook.

We're picking up speed. We're up. We're down. The wheels bump the ground briefly, and then we're up again. An empty feeling hits me in the pit of my stomach. I don't want to be airsick. I try to put that feeling out of mind.

"Hell, it's just a light drizzle," Slade says.

"Yeah." It's good to agree with a man every once in a while if you want to get him to do what you want.

"If you want," Slade shouts, "after a while, I'll do some Eights on Pylons and Chandelles for you."

"Tell us about the parachutes first," I say.

"I told you, don't worry about it. What do I have up here? A couple of worry-warts? I tell you, there's nothing to a flight like this. I do it a couple of times a day and nothing has ever happened to me yet."

"Well then, let's consider the laws of probability."

I look for some verbal support from Lew, but he doesn't say anything.

"What do you want to know about? I don't know nothing about probability. I quit school in eighth grade to go earn money for my family."

Tyrannized by the system, I think. Made to slave in the sweatshops. "What about the parachutes?" I ask.

"What about them?"

"What do I do if I need to use it?"

"You won't need to use it."

"What if?"

"I don't have much to tell you about them. I never had to jump from a plane in my life. Just remember not to pull the ripcord until you're free of the plane. If you pull it too soon, you might get messed up in the propellers or something."

"Get free of the plane."

"Right."

I tap Lew on the shoulder to make sure he's paying attention.

"And when you land," Slade continues, "hang loose, keep real loose and roll."

"Hang loose, keep real loose and roll."

"Right."

"I'd like to be stiff now," Lew says.

Slade looks at my partner. "There might be some bourbon in the back seat," Slade says. "I usually keep a bottle on hand for some of the businessmen I take up."

"Forget it," I say. I don't want Lew drinking on the job.

I'm a bit uneasy, but there is something to being off the ground, away from the earth, that is soothing to the spirit. From this height the exploitation of the workers seems minute indeed.

"Another thing to remember about parachutes," Slade says, "is that if you land in a high wind, you've got to run forward and collapse the chute. Otherwise you'll be dragged all over to kingdom come and that can kill you as well as anything else."

"Why don't we make it easy on ourselves and look for water," Lew says, more to me than to Slade, but I try to ignore it. All this talk about parachutes is making me uneasy. The roof that Lew and I practiced jumping from is high enough for me. Perhaps it would have been better if I sent Herdie along instead of me. Why should I risk my life? Herdie would do a good job. He always comes through in the clutch.

"Water ain't so easy either," Slade says, picking up on Lew's suggestion. "If the chute collapses over you, you'll drown. Best thing to do when floating down to water is to unbuckle the straps slightly—the leg straps—say, when you're about thirty or forty yards above the water, but you've got to be careful that you don't slip free of the harness too soon."

"Really?"

"Yeah. But as I say, you guys don't really have nothing to worry about. Just trust Winnie Mae and she'll take you where you want to go and back again."

I'm not in a particularly good mood, so I sit back in the seat and stroke the suitcase of explosives. In my lap the suitcase is an overgrown gray cat.

D-DAY—nearing target

". . . the proletariat alone is really the revolutionary class. The other classes decay and finally disappear in the face of modern industry." Maybe Lew is right. Maybe the revolution is behind the times. Maybe everything changes so quickly that revolution is impossible. I don't know. Confidence. That's the hardest thing to maintain.

"That's downtown Washington down there. Ain't that something?" Slade points out the sights to Lew, and Lew pretends to be interested, which for Lew is a pretty good act. A tough act to follow, as the announcer would say on television. "You don't know how lucky you are to be up here," Slade tells Lew, "instead of down there where the traffic is. You've got to be out of your mind to spend your whole life in traffic, and that's what people do every day in this town. I bet you don't have nothing like that in the Philippines."

Lew nods. "No, we don't. Except in Luzon. Luzon's pretty big, in its own way."

Lew looks calm, but I know he's jittery. I can tell by the way he plays with the guidebook, tossing it from hand to hand, flipping the pages, tapping on the cover.

"Who was that guy you mentioned? The ballplayer?" Lew asks.

"Clyde Klusewzki?"

"Yeah."

"Helluva ballplayer. I don't know what relation he is to me though."

Slade sidebanks the plane, and I can feel us going into an air pocket. I play with the straps on the suitcase in order to keep my mind off my stomach.

The suitcase, spotted with globs of red clay, is heavy, but really not heavy enough. What I want is a big bomb and a jet to drop it from. But that isn't what I want either. Too many innocent people will get injured. Maybe I need a 300-pound chemical bomb. Lots of them. Put everybody to sleep for a while. Perhaps in our dreams we can figure out where we are going, what we should do for each other. Still, there is something aesthetically pleasing about a blockbuster, something satisfying about a bomb hanging on a little parachute. I undo the straps, open the suitcase slightly, and peer in. There they are. My two little babies.

"Say, can I open one of the windows in here?" I ask.

"Yeah, but not too much."

"I won't get sucked out through the opening, will I?"

"What?"

"Forget it."

"You know, Slade, I really appreciate this flight," Lew alias Smith says. "I really couldn't see what America is like so easily. This is the best way."

"No traffic anyway," Slade says.

Lew is really laying it on pretty thick, but so much the better. No action without acting.

"Yeah, it's a great country all right," Slade says. "It's good no matter how you see it. But you need to get an overview before you can see it close-up."

"Yeah."

"See that big building across the Potomac? That's the Pentagon."

"I'd really like to fly over it," Lew says. "I've heard so much about it."

"You're the boss." Slade starts us toward the target. We are about to declare war upon War, war upon the Indiscriminate Use of Military Might.

I open the suitcase, but keep the cover up in such a manner that Slade can't see the contents. "I'm looking for a handkerchief," I explain. I am on the verge of a great act, perhaps the greatest of my life. I feel free. I feel liberated. I am above everything and everybody, not because I'm in some approximation of "The Spirit of St. Louis" a few thousand feet above the earth, but because I am breaking free from the chains of oppression, bigotry and militarism. A skywriter would have been the *pièce de résistance.* Let us all be free. Let us not be ruled by greed and by money. *The weapons with which the bourgeoisie felled feudalism to the ground are now turned against the bourgeoisie itself.*

"If you keep your eyes open," Slade says, "you'll see one of the largest office buildings in the world. It isn't in that guidebook I brought you, is it?"

"No," Lew says.

"It's a real old book. I'm sorry I don't have anything newer."

"Yeah." If Lew can keep Slade's attention focused on the sights, maybe I can drop the bombs without his knowing what's going on.

"How are you getting on back there?" Slade asks, meaning me.

"OK I guess. That air pocket got me."

"You'll be all right."

The rain has stopped completely now. Maybe the elements know I want to bring peace to the world.

"Like to see an Immelmann turn?" Slade asks.

"No, that's OK. Can we get any lower? I want my friend to see the Pentagon up close." Fidel Castro Ruz' Vladimir Ilich Ulyanov Che Guevara. Someday there will be a national holiday in my honor. At this moment of history, when I am poised to make a statement for the innocent dead, I want the names of rebels, revolutionaries, and outcasts thundering in my brains. Unfortunately, the only name that I can concentrate on is Immelmann.

"Hey, kid, wake up willya? Didn't you hear what I said?"

I glance up and see Slade staring at me in the mirror. "I said that I shook Eisenhower's hand once."

We are not yet over the center of the Pentagon. "Yeah, that's great," I say.

"What's that over there?" Lews asks, pointing toward the right. I wait for Slade to turn his head toward where Lew is pointing. When he turns his head, I lift the incendiary bomb out of the suitcase. Holding it by one hand, holding the bomb by its tail, all twenty pounds of it, I thrust it out of the window and let go. I know it's not going to hurt anybody, but that it will cause people to sit up and take notice.

Slade turns sharply. "Hey, what did you just do?"

"I didn't do anything. I was just getting rid of some garbage."

"He was just throwing out garbage," Lew repeats, supporting my story.

"*Garbage*!" Slade shouts. "You can't drop garbage on the Pentagon. There's a $50 fine for littering."

"I suppose there's no fine for littering foreign countries with the bodies of innocent victims!" I wait for the explosion, but I don't see anything go off.

"What in the hell is going on here?" Slade shouts. "What did you toss out of the plane? *I want to see what's in that suitcase.*"

Before things get out of hand, I quickly pass Lew the revolver and he points it at Slade's head, points it directly at the raggedy brown World War I helmet. "Just don't do anything foolish, Slade," Lew says.

"What are you? Communists or something?"

"I'm an anarchist."

"You're not going to get away with this," Slade says angrily. "Dropping garbage all over the Pentagon. Are you guys crazy or something?"

I remove the blockbuster from the suitcase and untwist the harness lines of its small parachute. In one way I am glad that the Pentagon is so large. It makes it more difficult to miss the target. It would really be an embarrassment if I missed the Pentagon altogether and ended up bombing something like a football field.

"Why didn't it go off?" Lew asks. "I paid enough for it. Can't Herdie do anything right?" All the while he keeps the gun pointed directly at Slade's head. I can't even remember if the gun is loaded or not.

"How am I supposed to know. I didn't build the thing,"

 I tell him. "Talk to your friend Herdie about it. He's your friend."

"He's your friend too," Lew snaps.

"You—you—you guys have been dropping a bomb out of my plane?" Slade says incredulously, his voice almost breaking. "I'm not going to let you get away with it. You Commies aren't going to do this to me."

"Anarchists," I correct him.

Slade won't listen. Instead he throws his Winnie Mae into a dive and Lew and I are momentarily thrown off balance. The blockbuster in my lap falls to the floor and the suitcase slides on top of it.

"I knew there was something wrong with you guys the moment I laid eyes on you," Slade yells. Lew grabs at the stick to recover Winnie Mae from her dive, but Slade's hands are far too strong for him, even though I have recovered enough from my spill to grab Slade around the head and throat. I throw his head back and Lew hits him on the skull with the revolver. I pommel Slade's head and face with my fists while Lew is desperately maneuvering the stick to bring us out of the dive. Everything in the plane slides and bounces, and my feet are tangled in the shroud lines of Herdie's blockbuster. God, why did Slade have to do this? Stupid guy. Can't he understand anything?

By the time the plane levels out, we are so close to the Pentagon that we might as well land on the heliport. "Hiya, gang, you're probably wondering what we're doing here." I can just imagine their faces. "Just thought we'd stop by and pay a surprise visit. Wanted to see how the war was going. Nothing to be alarmed about."

I don't know what I'm thinking of. I'm shaking like a leaf, with sweat pouring off my arms and hands. What am I doing here anyway?

"Take his hat off," Lew tells me.

"What?"

"Take his hat off."

"What are we going to do?" I remove the helmet from Slade's head and Lew lets him have it with the butt of the revolver.

"Stop it," I cry. "No!"

Two, three, four times. Just to be certain he'd be out. Slade slides down in the seat, his face covered with blood.

"It was only a partial dive," Lew says. "If he had thrown the plane all the way into a dive there would have been no chance at all for a recovery."

"What are you talking about? Look at him," I say. I take off my shirt and wrap it around Slade's head.

"I don't want to look at him, I don't want to think about it," Lew says.

"What did you do that for?"

"Shut up. Do you want us to get killed?" Lew is doing the best he can with the controls. "We're still in the air, aren't we?" Both of us are shaking and neither of us knows what to do. I don't have a contingency plan. "He'll be all right," Lew says.

"You hit him too hard."

"He's breathing, isn't he?"

"How do I know?"

"Look at him," Lew shouts, struggling with the stick. "Shut up. I don't want to stall us out."

When I look out the window there are hundreds of people on the ground, all of them running back and forth, pointing up at us.

"What are we going to do now?" Lew says, almost in tears.

"How do I know?"

"Don't yell at me. Don't you see I'm having trouble enough. I'm no expert aviator."

"Just take one thing at a time," I tell him, trying to find some calm in my voice. One thing at a time. That's going to be Rule Number One in the Handbook.

"I didn't want to hurt him," Lew says.

"I think I'm going to be sick." I stop short. The dives, bumps and rolls are too much for me. Any moment I think we're going to lose control of the plane. I try to vomit on top of the suitcase, but it's not easy to control something like that, especially at a time like this.

"Dammit," Lew says, "now you're making me sick too." The plane banks and lurches. Lew vomits too.

"Don't lose control of the plane," I mumble.

Lew has vomited into Slade's lap, but the plane, thank God, keeps gaining altitude. Winnie Mae smells like the inside of the bathroom after an all-night fraternity party.

Lew finally regains his breath. "We've got to get out of here," he whispers. Half of his phony mustache is hanging down.

"No," I say. "Not as long as I have this bomb. We've got to drop it."

"What are you, a fanatic?"

"I've got to get rid of it."

"But there are people down there," Lew says. His voice is husky, and mine is no better.

"I have to drop it," I say. "We can't leave Slade here with it." I push the suitcase aside and pick up the blockbuster. The only way I can cope with my panic is to concentrate on my plan. The parachute is stained with my breakfast.

"I can't work the stick this way," Lew says. "It's too awkward with Slade slumped all over everything."

"What can I do?"

"Move him."

He might as well tell me to fly as far as I am concerned. I put my hands under Slade's arms to get some idea of his weight. Moving him seems out of the question.

"Let's get rid of this before it's too late," I tell him. "As long as we're flying in some halfway decent way—I mean, we're not that far from our goal."

Lew plays with the control stick, pushing it tenderly,

lightly, slightly, teasing it, twisting it, while I untangle the lines of the blockbuster. It gives me something to do. If this bomb doesn't work, I'm going to kill Herdie.

"I've got an idea," Lew says. "Suppose we try an emergency landing on the heliport. We'll tell them that the pilot went mad while we were up here, and that we had to subdue him."

"Sure. And you know how long we'll be held for questioning? My great-grandfather didn't live that long. And what about the revolver?"

"Yeah, you're right."

"Sure I'm right."

"Well, it's the first time since this whole thing started," Lew says, gaining confidence at the controls.

Memo for the Handbook about private planes: Always get a pilot you can trust. Include a chapter on first aid. The Pentagon's walls are looming larger before us, with everything coming into our bombsights once again. Thank God for those fathers who are able to give their sons flying lessons. In the modern technological age, successful revolutionaries more often than not are going to come from the aristocracy. "You're doing great," I tell Lew. I don't feel that the praise is out of place. A little encouragement can only help matters.

"My back is killing me," he says. "I've got to get into the pilot's seat."

"OK, OK, I'll try." Slade is all dead-weight, but using all my strength I manage to force him to the right. Lew pulls Slade under him and partially crawls over him. With both of us sweating and straining, it takes us a good six or seven minutes to get Lew into the pilot seat. I don't know. I have no time sense anymore. I feel I am up against eternity. Slade is slumped over on the passenger side, leaning against the door. I shouldn't have got him involved. He doesn't deserve this grief.

"We should have changed to the Cessna when we had

 the chance," Lew says. "That's a plane I've been in before."

"Now you tell me," I answer, holding my stomach with my hands. It would have been easier to hijack a jet, but hindsight is as valuable to a revolutionary as it is to a baseball manager. A little while ago everything looked so simple. "Where is the gun? What did you do with the gun?"

"What difference does it make?" Lew croaks.

"We can't leave it on board. It's a clue."

"I think it's on the seat under Slade."

"I can't move him again."

"Let me think what I'm doing. . . . Wait a minute. Here it is, by my foot."

"Give it to me."

"Get it."

It's a long reach, but I manage to squeeze my arm between the seats and grasp the gun. If we had hijacked a 747, we'd have stewardesses to do this sort of thing for us.

Lew points to the glove compartment. "I bet there's a flight-instruction booklet in there somewhere."

Well, here goes. I pick up our baby blockbuster and dangle it out the window, directly over the Pentagon again. I don't want to let it go. I don't want to keep it in the plane. On the ground, people are running all around. Maybe I can just stand here and hold it outside until something better turns up.

"Let the damn thing go," Lew says. "Get rid of it."

"I can't!" I tell him. A sharp pain passes through my stomach, but then I let go. The blockbuster takes to the wind like a small bird leaving its nest for the first time, floating unsteadily, unevenly, dropping in the wind, haltingly and hesitatingly falling.

Lew lets out the throttle and I think I hear somebody shooting at our plane, but I can't be sure. Everything is happening too quickly, especially the pains in my stomach.

"What's happening?" Lew asks.

"I can't see anything." What difference does it make?

The revolution has begun. There's a small cloud of smoke in the distance below us.

"Do you see it?"

"I think it went off."

Behind us the Pentagon is getting smaller and smaller, though in my mind's eye it looms like a gigantic octopus with its corridors of red-taped, bureaucratic tentacles ready to strangle us.

"Where should we go?"

"How do I know?"

"Let's head for Canada," Lew suggests.

"We'll never make it."

"You're right. I can't keep this crate in the air much longer."

"Let me think a second."

"What about Slade?" Lew asks.

"I don't know." On top of it all, I have to go to the bathroom. When you read history books, do they ever tell you about the need for leaders to perform primary functions? No. It's always one great heroic deed after another, never a pause for rest. That's why most history is a pack of lies. Lies, lies, and more lies.

"Do you think Slade can identify us?" Lew asks.

"How should I know," I say. Lew's questions are beginning to annoy me. I don't have all the answers. I just want to live in a world where a guy can enter an elephant race without going to jail for it.

"You should have thought of these things," Lew says.

"Get off my back, willya?"

"I'm not on your back. Won't you understand? I'm losing control of the plane."

"Is it my fault the incendiary bomb didn't go off? I didn't build the thing."

"Now what? Are we going to fly around till we run out of gas or run into the side of a building?"

"Then go high. We're going to have to jump."

Slade lets out a groan. Even if we held the gun to his head, we couldn't trust him to land us.

"What does the instruction manual say about abandoning the plane?" Lew asks.

"I'm getting an ulcer."

"Chrissakes, help me."

"One thing at a time."

I hold onto the back of the seat with my hand, trying to steady myself. My kingdom, my kingdom, for a glass of ginger ale. I pick up the suitcase and slam it shut. I've got to get rid of the suitcase. I can't jump with a suitcase in my hands.

"Will you put your mustache on before Slade comes to?" I say. "Do you want him to have a good look at you?"

Lew rips the mustache off. "I'm through with this whole thing. Just don't let him come to."

"That's insubordination. I'll remember that."

Lew's face is completely drained of color. "Maybe we should give ourselves up."

"Are you crazy? We're not going to give ourselves up. Who gives them the right to drop bombs on people?"

There is no way for me to put a finger on my thoughts. The plane ride resembles a roller coaster that has lost its track. "Help me get Slade into the parachute," I say.

"How? How can I possibly do that, you stupid jerk? I'm trying to fly this plane!"

"Shut up." After much tugging and pulling and sweating, I manage to get a parachute strapped around the big guy. I can see that he is slowly reviving.

Lew is balancing the instruction manual on his lap. "You have to leave the plane head-first," he says. "And for God's sake, don't pull the rip cord too soon."

"What's too soon?"

"I don't know."

"I won't have time to count to ten."

"You're telling me."

"How about three?"

"Just remember to pull it."

"All right, all right, all right, all right." I think I'm going to die.

"And don't jerk the cord. Give it a steady pull."

"Come on."

"I'd rather stay with the plane," Lew says.

"You're going with me. Everybody and his uncle will be out looking for this plane."

"Try to land with your back to the wind."

Slade begins to stir.

"How will I know which way the wind is coming?"

"You'll know soon enough."

"I guess I will."

"Yeah."

"Where are we?"

"I don't know. I think we're in Delaware."

I sit back in the seat and wait for the Delaware farmlands to unroll below us. I wish I were dead. I wish I were dead. And Slade! What am I going to do about him?

"Let me try to land the plane," Lew says.

"Forget it. I don't want to be in it when it crashes."

"Then don't be in it. I want to land the plane."

"You're not going to." Memo for the Handbook: Firmness in all things, especially in decisions that affect your life, and it's hard to think of any decisions that don't.

"It's easy. I can follow the book. Reduce the throttle, turn on the carburetor heat, adjust the stabilizer . . ."

"Shut up, Lew. We're not going to do it. I'm tired of the whole mess. I just want to get out of here in one piece." I figure out how to prevent Lew from attempting to land the plane, so I take the flight manual and rip a few pages out, rolling them up.

"What are you doing?"

"Nothing."

"That isn't going to stop me."

I sit back and wait for Slade to regain consciousness. If he dies from this, I won't forgive myself.

"I feel terrible," Lew says.

"I've got to go to the bathroom." My left leg is shaking uncontrollably, but I sit in the seat, thinking of everything over and over. I've made my life or ruined it beyond repair, I can't figure out which. I find the bottle of bourbon that Slade has mentioned, and Lew and I take a couple of swallows to bolster our failing courage, but we're careful to leave enough to revive Slade. I force some of the liquor down him and slap him a couple of times. Please, God, let him be all right.

"Huh?" Slade is in bad shape all right. But he's a big man. He should be able to take a couple of hits in the head.

"Why did you get us into this?" Lew says.

"You wanted to do it too. You believe in the cause as much as I do."

"It's a mess," Lew says.

"Shut up."

"I'm scared. I'm scared stiff."

"What do you think I am? I'm scared too."

I suppose the land below us is rolling and beautiful. I suppose. I don't know anymore.

Slade's eyes begin to open, so I lean him against the door. "Look, Slade, can you hear me?"

"Huh?"

"Can you hear me?"

"Huh?"

"Look, Slade, do you understand me? I'm going to open the door and you're going out. You understand?"

Slade slowly opens his eyes.

"Just pull your rip cord and you'll be all right."

Slade's hands automatically go to the cord, but I stop them. "No, not now. Wait until you're free of the plane. Do you understand me? You're going to be all right."

"Let him stay in the plane," Lew suggests. "He'll be better off."

Slade doesn't say anything. His eyes are open, but he just stares at me. I pour what's left of the bourbon over his head, forcing him to swallow a few last drops. "OK, Slade, out you go. Just remember to pull your rip cord and you'll be all right." God, let him be all right, I think to myself.

Slade shakes his head and leans back, staring at the ceiling of the plane. "You bastards," he groans. I keep the gun pointed at his head in case he tries anything, but I can't hold the gun steady.

"I'm opening the door," I say, "so you better be ready. Get ready, willya?" As I open the door, Slade tries to grab me, but I'm safe behind the seat. Without thinking I press the trigger and the gun goes off, jerking my hand against the seat. The bullet tears through Slade's shoulder, catching him off-guard and toppling him out of the cabin into the Delaware sky. I watch with my mouth open and tears rolling from my eyes.

"Jesus, Jesus, Jesus," I say.

"Will you close the door," Lew yells.

"What?"

"Close the door."

My God, what have I done? I slam the door shut. The right side of the cabin and the seat next to the door are covered with Slade's blood.

The plane bolts forward as Lew opens the throttle, and I look back at the white canopy unfolding over Slade's head.

"I could have killed him, I could have killed him."

"You might have."

"I didn't mean to do it," I shout at Lew.

"Now what are we going to do?"

"Get away from here."

I put the revolver in my pocket, thinking how easy it is to kill somebody. How can it possibly be that easy?

"Pull yourself up on the shroud lines when you land," Lew says, staring at me, his eyes wide, his face in pain. "It'll help you break your fall."

"I heard you the first time," I tell him, taking the pages

 from the flight manual, rolling them up again, and lighting them.

"What are you doing?" Lew says.

I hold the paper to the suitcase until the suitcase catches fire. "I'm destroying the evidence."

"Put it out," Lew yells. "You're going to catch the whole damn plane on fire."

"That's the idea," I tell him. I throw the burning paper onto the front seat. "You better bail out with me before the plane explodes."

"I could have landed the plane."

"I'm leaving."

Lew throws open his door and dives out head-first. I go out the right way, but can't remember anything from the instruction book. The advice from him and Slade has evaporated in the atmosphere, evaporated with the image of my brother that has so certainly floated before me.

There's an empty feeling in the pit of my stomach. Empty and sour and harsh. I've got to remember to pull the rip cord. Six. Seven. Eight. I hit the end of the line with a bounce and a snap, swinging back and forth. It's slower now and steadier. The fiery plane is going down to some empty field, where I hope it will burn up with the evidence. I have to pull the lines on the high side. Pull. Below me is Lew's canopy, but I'm concentrating on myself, not on him. Everything in me feels hollow and shaky. I say that in Utopia there will be no parachutes. We will all float on the white canopies of our uplifted spirits.

February 28

My arms and legs are covered with bruises from being dragged by the chute and from not tumbling correctly, but that's not the worst part. Both Lew and Slade are in the hospital. Not the same hospital, of course, but at this point it makes very little difference. The FBI is moving in on me and I don't see how I have a chance.

According to the papers, Slade is in serious condition, though he does have a chance for recovery. Poor guy. His beautiful Winnie May has been destroyed. I suppose he has insurance on it. I hope so. At least I think I hope so. How do I know how I feel? I'm not a psychiatrist. Still, I'd like to send Slade some flowers, or a book about baseball, or something. But I can't take the chance.

Lew's in traction and I guess when he finally gets out of the hospital the police will be right there to pick him up. I'm sure he will never speak to me again. I wouldn't have left him in the field with a broken back if I had known. I did call an ambulance for him, though. I called anonymously from a phone booth, but I called just the same. I suppose Lew will confess the whole thing. Some friend. There ought to be some justice in this world.

And Lew isn't the only one who's turned against me. I've been trying to get in touch with Sally for the last couple of days, but she refuses to speak to me. She says she's tired of my schemes, and on top of everything else I think she's found a new boyfriend. Some biology major. I hope they're very happy together.

After I called the hospital for Lew, I called Sally. I managed to say, "Hello, Sally? Guess what." Then she slammed the receiver down, which I don't think is a good way to treat me. I finally sent her a message through Herdie, true, faithful Herdie. He's the one who finally got through to her and told me she's been spending a lot of time with the biology major. I hope to God he's a hydrophytographist or whatever and that they spend their time together lying around stagnant ponds. But I don't care. Is it my fault that it's so difficult to change the world? It seems to me that it should be easier for people to do good things.

If you want to know the truth, I'm spending most of my time in a beat-up station wagon I borrowed from one of Herdie's friends. The only thing I can say for it is that it's much more invigorating than being cooped up with an elephant. I drift around, buy hamburgers and stare at the calendar I got from one of the local banks.

I suppose it won't be long before they find me. The plane burned up, but I'm sure there are telltale things in the ashes. Also, Slade will be able to give them lots of leads and Lew will tell them everything, if he hasn't already done so. Maybe it's not so easy to speak when you're in traction. That would be a piece of luck, but I'm not that lucky.

I shouldn't be too hard on myself, though, because it's difficult to keep your spirits up in the back of a station wagon. I should look on the bright side of things. I didn't hurt anyone on purpose. Actually, if you want to look at it that way, I showed initiative, spunk, courage and I'm sure many other good qualities I'm not even aware of. I have to say that over and over again. Initiative, spunk, and courage. I will emphasize those qualities in my Handbook—that is, when I get back to editing it. The thing that really slows down my mind is that I'll probably be spending a lot of time in jail.

I have also been thinking about calling my parents, but what are they going to say? When I think about how upset they were over the elephant race, I can only imagine how they'll react to this. For a penalty, I think the electric chair will be the bare minimum.

I've tried to talk all of this over with Herdie, but he really doesn't understand. He wasn't up there with us. He sees it only from the standpoint of a scientist who created a bomb that worked.

Herdie tells me that now that we have momentum, we should keep up the frontal attack until the Establishment surrenders. His idea is to get some highly trained athletes to take over the White House. He's talking about getting into the White House and I can't even get back into college. A little grasp on reality, that's what Herdie needs. I told Herdie to call up my friend, Montgomery Frankel. I can't be responsible anymore. I'm too tired.

I guess what I really need is my disintegrating-ray gun so I could disintegrate myself and reappear when this has all blown over. My Flash Gordon disintegrating-ray gun. Maybe I need Flash Gordon, but he's not around. People are never around when you need them. I bet that's the way it's always been.